2·25

The identity of *Beowulf's* author and the exact date and place of its composition are unknown. A single copy of the poem, dated about the year 1000, survived Henry VIII's destruction of England's monasteries and was collected by Sir Robert Cotton. This copy was damaged, but not disastrously, in a library fire in 1731 and was finally placed in the British Museum in 1753. The Danish scholar Thorkelin had copies made of it in 1787 and published the whole of it for the first time in 1815. Originally untitled, it is named after its hero, Beowulf, and is divided into two parts: In the first part the young Beowulf battles the monster Grendel and Grendel's vengeful mother; in the second, an aged Beowulf kills a fire-breathing dragon but is himself mortally wounded.

No historic Beowulf is known to have existed, but some events described in the poem did take place in the sixth century. Early scholars tried to prove that more than one poet wrote the work, but it is now generally accepted that, like the *Iliad's* Homer, there was one composer of *Beowulf*, who took the stories, legends, and myths of his culture's oral tradition and bound them together with his own artistic vision. Written in England at least fifty years after the conversion of the Anglo-Saxons to Christianity, and perhaps much later, the poem is recognized today as the longest and greatest poem extant in Old English—yet it describes an ancient heroic society of Danes and Geats in Scandinavia; there is not one word about England, or about the people who come to be known as the English, in the poem.

Ask your bookseller for Bantam Classics by these British and Irish writers:

Jane Austen
J. M. Barrie
Charlotte Brontë
Emily Brontë
Frances Hodgson Burnett
Fanny Burney
Lewis Carroll
Geoffrey Chaucer
Wilkie Collins
Joseph Conrad
Daniel Defoe
Charles Dickens
Sir Arthur Conan Doyle
George Eliot
Ford Madox Ford
E. M. Forster
Kenneth Grahame
Thomas Hardy
James Joyce
Rudyard Kipling
D. H. Lawrence
W. Somerset Maugham
John Stuart Mill
E. Nesbit
Sir Walter Scott
William Shakespeare
George Bernard Shaw
Mary Shelley
Robert Louis Stevenson
Bram Stoker
Jonathan Swift
H. G. Wells
Oscar Wilde
Virginia Woolf

BEOWULF
and Other Old English Poems

Translated by Constance B. Hieatt

With an Introduction by A. Kent Hieatt

Revised and Enlarged Second Edition

BANTAM BOOKS
NEW YORK · TORONTO · LONDON · SYDNEY · AUCKLAND

BEOWULF AND OTHER OLD ENGLISH POEMS
A Bantam Book

PUBLISHING HISTORY

*First edition published by The Odyssey Press / The Bobbs-Merrill
Company, 1967*
Bantam Revised Classic edition / January 1983
2nd printing . . . September 1988

ISBN 0-553-21347-4

Published simultaneously in the United States and Canada

*Bantam Books are published by Bantam Books, a division of Bantam
Doubleday Dell Publishing Group, Inc. Its trademark, consisting of the
words "Bantam Books" and the portrayal of a rooster, is Registered in
U.S. Patent and Trademark Office and in other countries. Marca Regis-
trada. Bantam Books, 1540 Broadway, New York, New York 10036.*

PRINTED IN THE UNITED STATES OF AMERICA

O   11 10 9 8 7 6 5

Contents

Preface to the Second Edition

This version of *Beowulf* is obviously not intended for an audience of scholars of Old English, for no translation can be a substitute for the original. Nor is it a trot for graduate students struggling to reach that eminence: there are already enough more-or-less literal translations, such as that of E. T. Donaldson, to serve their purposes. My aim has simply been to produce a readable translation for adult readers and students who do not read Old English. A selection of shorter poems has also been included as some indication both of the quality and variety of Old English poetry and of its coherence as a body of literature. While all the shorter poems are quite different from *Beowulf* (and, in most cases, from each other), each has particular similarities, and all together can give a reader an idea of the literary context in which that great poem belongs.

Since readability was a primary objective, I have had to take some liberties in rearranging sentences and rephrasing, although I have tried to be as faithful to the text as possible. Those who use the translation as an aid in understanding the Old English are warned that, for example, what is an adverb in the original may turn up as an adjective in a rearranged structure. I have also discarded a few minor details, especially some that puzzle even specialists, but more of these obscure references remain than in the first edition since they may be felt to add to the amplitude of the felt "background."

Certain of the poetic embellishments (although not as many as in some translations) have also been sacrificed, since this a prose translation. Working in prose cannot really be described as a decision since I never seriously considered verse: it is my conviction that a verse translation may or may not be a good poem, but it is not the *same* poem. The qualities that remain the same in a translation are those of theme and overall structure, and greater verbal accuracy is possible in a prose translation, where a faithful rendering of the meaning (including certain verbal elements that can be seen as structural) is not obscured by the exigencies of a superimposed verse form. The shorter poems are, of course, generally more lyric, and thus lend themselves less easily to prose translation. But even here it still seemed preferable to render their content as clearly as possible without the obscuring effect of an alien (or pseudo-archaic) verse convention.

There are two apparent exceptions: *The Seafarer* is also given in Ezra Pound's brilliant verse translation, or adaptation, and *The Battle of Brunanburh* in Tennyson's rendition. If the reader will compare these poems with the prose translations, he may judge for himself some of the different advantages of prose and verse in translation.

As in the first edition, *Beowulf* has been divided into units approximating the "chapters" to which modern readers are accustomed. These have, however, been slightly rearranged and divided into the numbered divisions actually indicated in the manuscript. These may not seem the "logical" places for narrative divisions to a twentieth-century audience and there is no way of knowing whether they originated with the poet—nor are all the numerals present in the manuscript. However, *Beowulf* is not a twentieth-century narrative, and the division into what are known as "fitts" was, at least, made in Anglo-Saxon times and thus constitutes more-or-less contemporary evidence for the original audience's perception of structure.

Preface

In revising—and adding to—these translations, I have aimed at improving their fidelity to the "effect" of Old English poetry, as well as fidelity to the "meaning" of words and constructions translated. I have, therefore, paid careful attention to the impact of verbal patterns, including those suggested by etymology. In the case of the shorter poems, I have made an extra effort to improve the rhythmic effect of the prose: it is still prose, but the effect intended is one with a relationship to the rhythms of Old English verse. Those who know the field will understand if I say that the model is more nearly Ælfric than Caedmon.

Like the translations themselves, the notes were composed with a nonspecialist audience in mind. In general, I have given a note only where it seemed to me that the reader might be confused without it. I hope that the introduction will clear up many questions before they arise: a reader coming to Old English poetry for the first time should certainly be urged to read the introduction first.

I am fortunate in being able to include an introduction by my husband, A. Kent Hieatt, who has had much experience of teaching Old English poems in translation. Like the translations, the introduction has been revised for this new edition. I am grateful to him and to a number of other scholars who have read my work in one form or another for suggestions for its improvement—most of which were accepted. I owe a great debt of gratitude to other scholars and teachers for other reasons, of course, but most of all to John C. Pope. I would have dedicated the book to him if it had not seemed an inadequate offering.

CONSTANCE B. HIEATT

The University of Western Ontario
August 1982

Introduction

All of the poems which are translated in this collection reached the form in which we now have them between the seventh and tenth centuries. They were composed in Old English, or Anglo-Saxon, which was the earliest form of our language, preceding Middle English, which was, for instance, the speech of Geoffrey Chaucer (ca. 1340–1400). The small group of remarkable Old English poems and prose works that survives is the earliest body of literature in any of the vernaculars that have developed into the modern languages of Europe.

Beowulf (summary of story on p. xx), the longest and most important poem here, concerns famous deeds supposedly performed in an age long before that of the poet, among Germanic tribes living near the European homeland from which the Anglo-Saxons, another Germanic folk, had come to England. Most scholars believe that it was composed by a single author in the eighth, ninth, or tenth century. The Christianity of the poet's England was still strongly influenced by pagan habits of thought. *Beowulf* may come from the far north of England—Northumbria—but more probably from Mercia, directly to the south of this.

We should not know of *Beowulf* at all if a single manuscript of it had not survived the expropriation of the monasteries, with their libraries, by Henry VIII in the sixteenth century, and a disastrous library fire in 1731. This manuscript apparently dates from the tenth century. Charred at the edges by the fire, it continues to deteriorate year by year. An edition of it prepared by the Dane Thorkelin from copies made in 1787 preserved many words which have since disappeared from the original, but this edition was burned in the British bombardment of Copenhagen in 1807. The original transcriptions—one by a professional scribe, the other by Thorkelin—fortunately survived.

The history of *Beowulf*'s physical preservation is, then, something of a cliff-hanger. The poem itself has been systematically studied only during a recent part of its long existence. As a consequence of this study the estimate of this work's significance has undergone mutations almost as sensational as the manuscript's survival of the burning of Robert Cotton's library. It is now almost customary to begin writing about it by condemning earlier commentators. This is possibly as it should be, for *Beowulf* even today is the most drastically misunderstood of all the monuments of English literature. Furthermore, it is so difficult to say what the work really amounts to that it is easiest to begin by smothering in the cradle some easily conceived false ideas that arise from mating it with quite different kinds of poems, or from judging it by literary standards irrelevant to its highly individual kind of life.

One of the most influential essays ever written about *Beowulf* states absolutely that it is a lyric, not a narrative, poem. This is possibly intentional exaggeration, but what J. R. R. Tolkien (see Bibliography) probably meant was that the poem is a tissue of oblique allusions and highly stylized elegiac passages intended to build a particular atmosphere and a particular feeling about life, more than it is a straight narration of a series of events in the life of a hero. This claim is surely true. *Beowulf* cannot be considered an epic like the *Iliad*. Moreover, in spite of its calamitous ending this poem is not a "tragedy" in the sense in which the *Iliad* or Sophocles' *Oedipus the King* or *Hamlet* is a tragedy, or in the sense in which Aristotle said tragedies ought to function. For a probable majority of specialists its hero has no specific tragic flaw precipitating his downfall; his only flaw is the most general one that he belongs to humankind and is subject to our common fate. On the other hand *Beowulf* is not simply a myth or a piece of folklore, for it is a product of sophisticated literary calculation. And it is not an allegory of good and evil, as so much medieval literature is, for the warfare that forms its background is not an *abstract* illustration of ethical problems; some of this strife is certainly historical, and much more may be.

One reason that *Beowulf* is difficult to describe as a piece of literature is that it had no successors and that nothing like it survives. It is true, of course, that the very local Germanic language in which it was written has gone on from strength to strength until in its modern forms it is the most important language in the world; but the great body of partly heathen, partly Christian Germanic poetry and prose to which *Beowulf* belongs became a closed system long ago.

The Germanic peoples of the Dark Ages had a shared tradition of oral composition stretching from Austria and Northern France north and west to Scandinavia and Iceland. If we consider this body of works in terms of what was written down and survived, we may say that it begins with Old English literature (seventh–eleventh centuries), continues in the material of the Icelandic Edda and sagas (eleventh–thirteenth centuries) and in some less important German and Scandinavian material, and closes with the Austro-German *Nibelungenlied* (ca. 1204). Efforts to revive this literature or imitate it have been interesting in themselves but have missed its true quality. The Germanic dragon slayer Sigemund of *Beowulf*, for instance, some of whose attributes are those of the Sigurd of the Icelandic *Volsungasaga*, and of the Sifrit of the *Nibelungenlied*, is apparently revived in the Siegfried of Wagnerian opera, but Wagner's Siegfried and Brunhilde share the effect of some early Germanic literature only at a kind of mythical, preliterary level. The development of the narrative and stylistic traditions of later English and all other poetry and fiction really lies outside the influence of this Germanic literature. Even the Old English alliterative verse forms scarcely survived after the century of Chaucer, the fourteenth, when they came back briefly into surviving writings in the highly altered form of *Sir Gawain and the Green Knight* and some other poems in the north and west of England. That was nearly the end, except, perhaps, for the point that English poetry alliterates more to this day than poetry does in most other languages.

Even within the total body of early Germanic literature, *Beowulf* stands by itself in many important respects. Icelandic saga, for instance, is severely objective in its narrative: authorial comment and point of view are so muted that the modern reader is likely to lose his bearings. *Beowulf*, on the other hand, is commentary through and through, in several senses. Sometimes the commentary is very sly, in the sense that one section of the story inconspicuously contrasts with or parallels another, or that an interpolated story or allusion has some kind of many-layered reference to the main action. At other times the commentary is very straightforward, as when the character King Hrothgar makes ethical pronouncements worthy of another Dane, Polonius, or when the author himself is performing one of his bracing exercises in differentiating the sheep from the goats. (He consigns nicors, dragons, ungenerous kinglets, cruel queens, Cain-descended beings, and cowardly retainers to darkness, mist, slime, fens, caves, and perdition with a heart-warming gusto and rhetorical amplitude; the rest of us, on the other hand, are made to seem sons of light. The author's aims are really far from being simpleminded, but he is against evil with the muscular conviction of a muckraking newspaper.)

Here, certainly, the objectivity of Icelandic saga furnishes no parallel, either to *Beowulf* or to most of the rest of Old English poetry, which almost always shares in this militant glorification of good over evil; some Old English poems, in fact, wallow rhetorically in this contrast. But even if we narrow the focus from Germanic literature in general to Old English literature in particular, the rest of this highly interesting Old English poetry is of only a little help in understanding what is literarily most important about *Beowulf*.

What other Old English poetry most obviously shares with *Beowulf* is a system of versification. In this system, end rhyme almost never appears. Unless a line is defective, it has four beats or, technically, "lifts"; the line itself consists of two "verses," between which there may or may not be a pause; and the sound at the beginning of the syllable carrying the third lift also appears at (i.e., alliterates with) the beginning of the first lift, or of the second lift, or of both of them, but never at the beginning of the fourth lift (alliterating lifts are italicized here):

Swa be*g*nornodon   *G*eata leode
1   2   3   4

*hl*afordes *hr*yre,   *h*eorth-geneatas;
1   2   3   4

cwædon thæt he *w*ære   *w*yruld-cyninga,
1   2   3   4

*man*na *mild*ust   ond *mon*-thwærust,
  1   2   3   4

*leod*um *'lith*ost   ond *lof*-geornost.
  1   2   3   4

In the feet (iambs, trochees, anapests, dactyls) of most poems likely to be familiar to the reader, the number of unaccented syllables is theoretically constant, but in Old English poetry the number of unaccented syllables between the lifts typically varies. In the final five lines of *Beowulf,* which are quoted above, there is no syllable at all between the last two lifts in the last two lines. This kind of verse was traditionally recited aloud, not read silently. A widely accepted theory suggests that the note of a harp was used to substitute for spoken syllables at some points in the pattern. For instance, in the first line above, such a note (indicated below by a rest substituting for a musical quarter note) probably supplied the first lift. According to the most popular theory today,[1] each quarter of a line with its lift was heard as a measure in 2/4 musical time, here indicated by quarter and eighth notes:

Aside from versification, certain shared stylistic traits (discussed below) make *Beowulf* and all other Old English poems sound superficially rather alike. Nevertheless, *Beowulf* remains significantly different. *Widsith* only alludes to some of the characters in *Beowulf* and their deeds. The only other complete poem in Old English that deals with the deeds of Germanic heroes is *Deor,*

---

[1]That of John C. Pope, most simply explained in *Seven Old English Poems,* edited by him (New York: W. W. Norton, 2nd ed., 1981).

but this is a short lyric. It is a notable statement of the
transitory nature of earthly life, but it is not, as *Beowulf*
is, a long narrative *about* these deeds. *The Wanderer* and
The Seafarer are similarly short, wonderfully evocative
lyrics, among the best and most famous in Old English,
but they are not at all concerned with traditional Ger-
manic heroes. The deeds of such heroes are related in
other Germanic languages of the Middle Ages, but, as
was indicated, the poems or prose works in which these
relations appear are so different from *Beowulf* that they
do not much help our understanding of the poem as a
work of art. On the other hand, the Old English *Maldon*
and *Brunanburh* are outstanding narrative poems, like
Beowulf, but they are much shorter, and each of them is
about one battle within the immediate historical range
of the poet, not about some semimythical past. *Waldere*
and *Finnsburh* do enter that past, but are merely tanta-
lizing fragments of lost longer poems. Other Old En-
glish poems are built on far different material borrowed
from outside the Germanic world. The Old Testament
is drawn on and adapted in the poems *Genesis, Exodus,*
and *Daniel,* and in *Judith,* a very powerful fragment.
Caedmon was inspired to compose a Creation-hymn
that is similar to the one reported in *Beowulf.* (The
story is that Caedmon thought poorly of his own poetic
abilities. When he attended a feast at which each guest
was expected to chant a poem, he retired to a shed.
There an angel told him to compose this poem on the
spot, which he did.) Saints' lives from the Mediterra-
nean world appear in *Andreas, Elene,* and *Juliana,* and
the allegorized story of a non-Germanic miraculous
bird in *The Phoenix.* Besides other material from the
New Testament, the story and significance of Christ's
crucifixion is fervently rendered in *The Dream of the
Rood,* perhaps the most remarkable of Old English de-
votional poems.

Great as these poems are, none of them really

comes near what many students of the subject now recognize as the essential artistry of *Beowulf*, although there is one interesting qualification here: all these poems, whatever the subject, make use of some of the heroic habits of thought which *Beowulf* shares. For instance, the Cross, imagined as speaking in *The Dream of the Rood*, describes a Christ who is active and warriorlike in his crucifixion, which sounds like a battle:

> The young Hero—who was God almighty— stripped off his attire; strong and resolute, he mounted the high gallows, brave in the sight of many when he wished to free mankind. I trembled when the Warrior embraced me. . . . They drove through me with dark nails; the wounds are still visible, open signs of malice.

Christ's followers conduct his death rites as though they were Germanic warriors:

> There they took almighty God, lifting him from the heavy torment. . . . They laid the weary Warrior down and stood by the head of his body. There they watched the Lord of Heaven, and he rested there for a while, exhausted by the great ordeal. They began to make a sepulcher for him—warriors still within view of his bane—carving it out of bright stone, and in that they set the Ruler of triumphs. When they were ready to depart, exhausted, from the glorious Lord, they raised a song of sorrow, wretched in the evening-time: he rested there, with little company.
> We still stood there, weeping in that place for a long time. The voices of the warriors faded away. The body grew cold, fair dwelling of the soul.

It is only in two strictly speaking nonliterary respects that most Germanic narratives—Old English, Icelandic saga, the *Nibelungenlied*—share something important with *Beowulf*. A reader needs to know about these points in order to understand *Beowulf* itself. The first of these is the frequent similarity of narrative motifs— much the same heroes, much the same incidents—often appearing in widely separated times and places. The Germanic peoples seem to have inherited a common body of narrative, which is a key to understanding the often incomplete and puzzling allusions and interpolated stories forming a large part of *Beowulf*. The other feature that *Beowulf* shares with other Germanic narratives is an emphasis upon the ethical principle of loyalty to another—to friend, family, chieftain, tribe, or the company of all faithful Christians (one of the clearest illustrations of this principle is *Maldon*). The breaking of this bond through cowardice or treachery is considered singularly abominable; and personally executed revenge—no matter how long delayed, no matter how sanguinary—against the ones who harm one's associates is held to be obligatory for every man, unless he is to be shamed publicly and even to hate himself. A typical tragedy of the Icelandic sagas is that of the good and farseeing man who will not stir for small causes, even when his wife taunts him and his sons press weapons into his hands, but who, knowing he will sooner or later be murdered in turn, will kill coldly and kill again when this vengeful necessity of his manhood and fame is finally thrust upon him by the folly of others. In the same way, the pathos of the *Nibelungenlied* lies in the working out of a devious pattern of mutual vengeance through hecatombs of frightful slaughter. The author himself sees that loyalty so understood is self-defeating, but he shows us no alternative. The Old English poems adapting Old Testament materials often center around much the same idea of vengeance: for example, the heroine of *Judith* cuts Holofernes' throat as a revenge for the Israelites, Satan revenges himself on God by attempting to destroy mankind, and God revenges himself on the Egyptians for the sake of his chosen people.

Liberal opinion is, of course, in full flight from this general principle, although each of us must recognize its force, inwardly in himself and outwardly in the feud, in the vendetta, and in much of the history of our own country and the world. It seems clear that, in almost every part of the world, this principle has been the naturally accepted one, granted in any society organized tribally and in terms of bloodlines, especially where legal remedy is lacking. Loyalty and bloody deeds of vengeance are preoccupations in much of the world's literature, not least in the later, feudal Middle Ages, in which the division of Lancelot's or Tristram's loyalty between the queen whom he loves and the king whom he serves is a famous case in point. But Germanic story probably makes more of this doubtful ideal than does any other narrative tradition.

Beowulf, admittedly, shares in this doctrine of particular loyalties and of personal and social vengeance, and in the literary habit of extracting pathos from these patterns, but with a vital difference. In *Beowulf* alone these ideals appear in a partly sublimated and palatable form—institutionalized, so to speak, and harnessed into the service of a permanently acceptable view of man's lot, not of our primitive urges solely.

Beowulf's own loyalty, it is true, is literally tribal and familial. In the foreground of the story, the young hero, a nephew of the king of the Geats in Sweden, goes to the Danes, with whose kings he has connections, destroys the Dane-devouring monster Grendel, destroys Grendel's mother (who has executed an unlooked-for vengeance herself), returns to the Geats, serves his king and the latter's successors, becomes king himself, and in his old age kills and is killed by a dragon who had been destroying the Geats. In the background of the story, the hero is even caught up in self-destructive tribal war, just as certain loyal warriors of the *Nibelungenlied* or a wife-ridden Icelandic hero may be drawn into the execution of vengeance. Beowulf fights the Frisians because his rash king leads him among them; he fights the Swedes because his tribe has inherited a pattern of vengeance and countervengeance against them.

It is attractive to believe, however, that this pattern of personal and tribal loyalties is generalized. The *Beowulf* author's intention seems to be to define the preeminent man as such, who is generous and helpful to those around him and gains his fame by such acts. In the foreground he fights what seem to be the enemies of us all, not simply of his friend, his family, or his tribe. He fights the fundamental forms of evil and harm, the descendants of the life-destroyer Cain—Grendel and his mother, envious of all human joy—and then the fire dragon, full of anger against man. He ostensibly avenges the harm done to the Danes in the one case and to his own Geats in the other, but the forms against which the vengeance flows out seem to be mythical shorthand for what hurts all of us; they are not human enemies (as they are in most Germanic narratives) whose destruction might involve him in self-defeat or, as we say, in guilt. In other senses as well Beowulf is the one man in the poem who will *not* provoke the evils with which we hurt ourselves. He is the one who is not disloyal to his king, not treacherous towards his king's wife and son upon the king's demise, not ungenerous and murderous when he is a king himself, not cowardly—all things that others are guilty of in some dimension of the poem's curious allusiveness.

What is just as important, however, is that beyond all this he is not the bringer of a millenium, either, nor can anyone be, in the universe of the poem. The insistence upon the hero's ultimate overthrow is one of the work's most striking heritages from the body of Germanic narrative. Beowulf resists evil for a time, but what hurts us finally kills him as he is in the act of killing one of its forms. The two peoples whom he has principally benefited are both to be destroyed by their folly and others' vengeance. The ethical life of the poem, then, depends upon the propositions that evil can sometimes be truly identified, that those who fight it are good and those who conquer forms of it are wonderful, but that finally the evil that is part of this life is too much for the preeminent man, as it is for all the rest of us. The object of our vengeance ought to be to destroy what hurts all of us, not to perpetuate more that is hurtful; but, justly maintaining that after all our efforts doom is there for all of us, the *Beowulf* is enabled to capitalize on the mighty pessimism of Germanic story.

The transmutation of Germanic mores from personal vengeance to the fight against evil depends partly on the Christianity of the author (see below), but the ethical views expressed above can be taken very seriously by many people today, whatever their religious belief, so that *Beowulf* remains morally very much alive. Two other dangers for the life of the poem, however, proceed from the author's method of embodying these notions in his poem. These are what usually bother the modern reader on first contact. They are elementary matters, but they must be defined in a somewhat roundabout way.

Readers in this century are accustomed to one kind of literary discourse, and one way of looking at the world through fiction, which might be called literary or moral realism. We tend to read fictional narratives from whatever culture in terms of this standard, which is usually first absorbed from novels and other fiction of the last two hundred years. What makes Homer's Achilles delightful to many of us is that, in spite of his millenial distance from us, he is immediately believable because he is a mixture of qualities—a supreme fighter, but childishly uncooperative and sulky; utterly vengeful and then, suddenly, amenable to fellowfeeling for his enemy Priam and to a sense of the total human plight. Contrariwise, in similar fictional situations we have learned from modern literature to recognize a completely good or bad character as unsatisfactory. He is a dishonest creation because no one is "really" like that, and he is a nonfunctioning inhabitant of his fictional world because his creator has not employed the chief resource of the modern imagination: the sense of the complexity, the "liveliness" of life. A contemporary reader often has a very good nose for this feature of a bad novel. Such a reader is likely to apply the standards of realistic fiction to *Beowulf* and to conclude that its hero is an incredible superman, or that he is as little revelatory of the true springs of human conduct as is the story of George Washington and the cherry tree. The two objections are, then, (1) that the *Beowulf* author is dishonest, or a dupe of his primitive milieu, in foisting upon us a figure of a kind which we shall never meet in our waking life, and (2) that the poem has no life to it because its main figures are puppets—Beowulf all light; Grendel, the latter's mother, and the dragon all in darkness. To put it another way, many who read *Beowulf* for the first time find it difficult to come to terms with its narrative as such, even though they may be prepared to admit that the *Beowulf* poet removed the curse of blood-guilt by opposing his hero to the supernatural enemy rather than to human ones. Many modern readers, in fact, would prefer not to admit even that, but to think that the author was too primitive in his thinking to have any choice in the matter, a harsh opposition between a perfect hero and an evil dragon or the like being the only fictional formula imaginable in those crude days. (This, by the way, is quite untrue; the

background of the poem is full of the alternative for-
mula of heroes face to face in dubious battle.)

In any case, the two difficulties are finally easy to
understand because they are so elementary. If the poem
really suffers from them, it can be left to historical
study, like the tenth-century Continental *Waltharius,*
in which the Germanic heroes are of such thin cardboard
that the story turns to farce. But these objections are
almost certainly irrelevant in the case of *Beowulf.*

Almost everyone touched by modern culture agrees
today that an art is possible beyond realism, embodying
our deepest subliminal urges and convictions, of the
kind which has been embodied in myth and which
appears to us in dreams. People agree to this, generally
because they have been told it so often, but many of
them must not understand what is really entailed, be-
cause, along with what is remarkable, so much merely
modish and shallow art has made its mark under the
aegis of this proposition. The truth of the proposition
itself, however, is not in doubt. The most important
and widespread example in Western culture is proba-
bly the Mass. In one sense it is art, and drama; however,
its moving effect on those for whom it is celebrated
depends not upon realistic features but upon its won-
derfully artful summoning up of feelings about willing
self-immolation, the participants' unity in the Self-
Immolator, and His exemplary chieftainship over them.
It is unnecessary to cite examples from modern litera-
ture, drama, or art, or from myths provided by the
anthropologists, for every reader can probably supply
his own.

Beowulf's artistic embodiment is mainly of the sort
described. It is only a subsidiary point that some realis-
tic touches are in fact given to the hero (to call a man
drunk to his face at the mead-bench, as Beowulf does,
argues a heedless, if sanctioned, forthrightness that
would have done credit to the historical American Fa-

ther of his Country in one of his tempers). The main point is that *Beowulf* mobilizes mythical feelings and creates a mythical picture of life in a supremely artful way. The artfulness is very important. A local myth about life and death, heroic self-sacrifice, and final defeat by the enemy of us all is simply material for the original believers and the anthropologist no matter how true it is to our subliminal experience, unless it has something else to validate it as an independent work of art. Theoretically, this "something else" may be the realistic treatment that we first spoke of. Probably, however, only the best modern historical novels succeed in following the canons of realism and in giving psychological and material particularity to mythical material; in being so treated, their myths perhaps become something else. Considerations of this kind of particularity and realism are only marginal in our poem. Its artfulness is largely a matter of structure and style.

Structure

Only an early Germanic audience would have come naturally by the kind of information that elucidates *Beowulf*'s structure. We may take a particular example and then examine the whole structure of the poem summarily.

One of the apparently most confused sequences in *Beowulf* is what happens between the hero's defeat of Grendel (p. 23) and (on the next night) the fatal carrying off by Grendel's maddened mother of the beloved counselor Aeschere (p. 35). In the foreground of action there is no particular difficulty for the reader: the Danes and the Geatish visitors follow the wounded Grendel's spoor to the mere beneath which he has sunk; they return exulting to the hall; they feast; they retire; Grendel's mother comes and carries off Aeschere. But interlarded with all this, and taking up far more space, are the following: (1) during the return to the hall, a recitation of the deeds of the Germanic dragon-slayer Sigemund and a statement of how he and Beowulf differ from the evil king Heremod; (2) at the feast, a recitation of how a Danish princess named Hildeburh, having been married to Finn of the Frisians in order to establish peace with that people, had to see her Danish brother and her son murdered in a new outbreak between Danes and Frisians (later a Danish retainer murdered her husband in revenge, and she was taken back to Denmark); (3) at the feast, a speech in which Queen Wealhtheow of the Danes assures her relative Hrothulf that she looks forward with confident serenity to his helpful attitude towards her sons after their father, King Hrothgar, will have died; (4) at the feast, a comparison of the treasures there bestowed on Beowulf with other treasures taken by one Hama, who underwent the envy of Ermanaric. Among Beowulf's treasures is a ring whose subsequent history is given (it passed to Beowulf's king, Hygelac; it was then lost in the battle with the Frisians when Hygelac was killed).

All of this sounds narratively confused—the kind of fiddling irrelevance that made earlier students of *Beowulf* believe that the work was an accretion of many hands, not the product of one author. But the situation is not really confused at all, if one knows what the author and his early audience almost certainly knew. The first point to be held in mind is that the author is partly concerned with foreboding: at the feast just before they retire it is said of the guests, "They did not know the doom, grim destiny, which many of the nobles would meet." Then they go to bed and Grendel's mother carries off Aeschere to her den to feast on him. Some sort of contrast between that and the joy of the feast is one of the things intended. What a contemporary audience would have been likely to know makes very good sense out of the apparent irrelevancies.

Wealhtheow, the queen, and her husband King Hrothgar had two sons and a daughter. After Hrothgar's passing, Hrothulf, instead of justifying Wealhtheow's expectations ("I expect that ... he will well repay our children"), deposed and killed one of the sons, as we hear from elsewhere. We know that the daughter, Freawaru, has been betrothed to the chief of another tribe in order to end a feud; Beowulf predicts (p. 54) that the peace will not last, but that a retainer of one side, inflamed to vengeance by a friend, will attack the other. Her sorrow, in other words, and the situation between the two peoples, will strongly resemble the sorrow of that other bereaved Danish princess, the wife of Finn, and the situation between the Danes and the Frisians as recited at the feast. The future situation, in fact, will probably be worse. We judge from another source that it is the tribe of Freawaru's husband that will eventually burn down Heorot, the very hall in which this feast is given. Furthermore, the future of the ring which is presented to Beowulf (Wealhtheow says to Hrothgar, "Rejoice. . . . Be gracious to the Geats, remembering how many gifts you have gathered from far and near") is an earnest of "grim destiny": Beowulf's king, wearing it, loses everything, life included, in the disastrous battle of his Geats with the Frisians.

Not all of the significances here are so bitter: Hrothulf stands in contrast to Beowulf, who after the death of his own king protects the heir and the queen instead of usurping the kingdom as he could easily have done. Perhaps Ermanaric stands in the same relation to Beowulf, for he is a type of the evil ruler in this poem and elsewhere. The story of Sigemund the dragon slayer, however, which in the action constitutes simply praise of Beowulf for destroying Grendel, has darker tones: Sigemund ventures beneath a stone to kill a dragon; so, later, will Beowulf venture. But Sigemund's dragon guards a treasure having a death-curse for him who takes it, and Beowulf's slaying of the treasure-guarding dragon will be at the expense of his own life. That treasure, too, is accursed. The song in praise of Beowulf's victory, then, is in part an anticipation of his own end.

It follows from all that has been said, therefore, that the series of apparently wandering interruptions in the action between the death of Grendel and the carrying off of Aeschere are repeated reminders to the general tune of "They did not know the doom, grim destiny, which many of the nobles would meet": feasting and joyful, the hall companions do not imagine that the enemy from the outer darkness will immediately renew the assault and carry off one most important among them; in a larger sense, the elated actors in the drama do not realize that the Danes are to undergo later repeated blows of fate, that the hero will be destroyed, and, in fact, that his destruction will signify the beginning of the end for his tribe, the Geats. In the largest sense of all, an elegiac view of life is powerfully generated. The mood, if not the substance, is the same as in the story quoted by the Old English writer Bede in his *Ecclesiastical History of the English People*: man's life is like the flight of a bird, which, buffeted by a storm, flies into a bright hall where men are feasting, and then flies directly through an opposite window into the darkness again.

The author seems to follow this method throughout. Story, brief allusion, or event looks backward and forward or at the human lot so as to give a strong emotional direction to any particular part of the narrative and to tie the whole together in extremely complex ways. One need not fear the complexity, however, since the method resembles the associative ones in a number of modern authors who depend on our common stock of knowledge for the raw material of their effects. A reference to George Washington and the cherry tree would not be illuminating to an Old English audience but is to us; and a modern poet who, desiring to create a sinister effect in connection with these associations, followed on with the Washington Tidal Basin, gifts of cherry trees from the Japanese, and Pearl Harbor, would probably impress the *Beowulf* poet as very subtle after the progression of ideas had been explained to him. While the reader of a translation cannot fully appreciate the powerful atmospheric quality of the style in rendering these allusions forceful, he can nevertheless see for himself how the structure of the poem directs thought and feeling into deep channels. The original audience would probably have seen the poet's points immediately. From parallel references in the *Beowulf* itself, in the Old English poems *Deor, Widsith,* and *Finnsburh,* in the material of the Icelandic Edda and sagas, and in the *Nibelungenlied,* we know that many of our poet's allusions were to a common stock of stories and heroes known throughout the Germanic world.

Having considered one sequence in detail, we pass on now to a summary examination of the total structure of *Beowulf.*

We have a funeral at each end of the poem. *Beowulf* opens with the mysterious arrival from the sea of the culture hero of the Danes. His name, Scyld Scefing, is given to them ("Scyldings" is a modernized equivalent of a word often used for the Danes in the Old English original); "Scefing" may suggest a sheaf of wheat—in which case he is a fertility figure as well. His funeral ship bears him out to sea, again mysteriously; certainly it looks forward to the funeral pyre of Beowulf, that other benefactor of peoples, upon a headland at the conclusion. The poem falls into two parts: the hero's exploits in youth as a generous helper of the Danes, and his adventure in age in doing his best to benefit his own tribe in Sweden. But the first part looks forward to the misfortunes of the Danes—the dissension and sorrows of the rulers, the final destruction of their great hall Heorot by flame, as already suggested. The first part also conveys, in its allusions to the behavior of Unferth and Hrothulf, the counterpoint of misdemeanor against which Beowulf stands out. And, most powerfully in the lay sung in celebration of his first victory, but also elsewhere, it suggests the ruinous ambiguity of his final victory and the general elegiac bent of the work. Throughout, the behavior of evil rulers like Heremod contrasts pointedly with the actions of Beowulf, the later king. Between the first and second parts falls the great speech of the aged Danish king, Hrothgar. It is rich in pronouncements. His prescriptions for manhood and kingship look backward into history and forward into the career of Beowulf; his prohibitions are similarly allusive; and his statement of the common fate looks forward to Beowulf's end and the ensuing, predicted doom. In the second part symmetry is given to Beowulf's career by his slaying of the dragon, but the victory, in the descending arc of life, is ideally sacrificial: he gives his life for his people.

The suggestions of ruin here are overpowering. The dragon is guarding the treasure of a vanished race; we hear the lament of its last member. We realize that the end of Beowulf's race is also in view. The pattern of loyalty, always firmly held by the hero himself, is broken. Of twelve chosen warriors only one, the virtuous Wiglaf, helps Beowulf in his final need. The vultures of tribal vengeance will now come home to roost: the Frisians whom the Geats had attacked under Hygelac will attack the Geats; the tribe will now be defenseless before the onslaught of the neighboring Swedes, with whom there is an enduring feud. The horrible inevitability of thrust and counterthrust in these patterns of loyalty and vengeance comes home to us as to the original audience of Germanic story only if we are allowed to stand and count the bloodthirsty blows as the author enumerates them: Haethcyn, brother of Hygelac of the Danes, had captured the wife of Ongentheow, king of the Swedes; Ongentheow and his band had then killed Haethcyn. Hygelac attacked Ongentheow, and Eofor, a member of the Geatish band, killed Ongentheow; Hygelac gave his daughter to Eofor as a reward. Ongentheow's son Onela was then on the Swedish throne. His brother's sons, Eanmund and Eadgils, exiled for rebellion, were befriended by Hygelac's son Heardred, who had succeeded to the Geatish throne after Hygelac's death among the Frisians. Onela attacked and killed Heardred. Beowulf, now king, inherited the feud and helped Eadgils, who, thus aided, killed Onela and became king of the Swedes.

There is at the time of Beowulf's death further rich cause for mutual extermination. Eanmund, the brother of Eadgils, had been killed by one Weohstan, a retainer of Onela. Who, from the present Swedish king Eadgils' point of view, inherits the bloodguilt from Weohstan? None other than Weohstan's son Wiglaf, the loyal young warrior of the dragon fight, who is now to be king of the Geats. As usual with the *Beowulf* author, this final calamity is hinted at, not expressed baldly; and the general parallel between it and the troubles of the Danes is also left for the reader to guess.

Style

The main tradition of Germanic verse was oral. A professional, called a *scop*, spoke or chanted narrative verses on festive occasions, as happens in the narrative of *Beowulf*. As noted, his chanting may have been accompanied by the sound of a harp (see p. xvi). When, for instance, Caedmon left the table in embarrassment, a harp was being passed around as an adjunct to each guest's poetic contribution. The harp may have been plucked only occasionally, to help out the meter; exactly how it was used—if it was used—is unclear. A number of habitual phrases—bardic formulae—made it possible for him to improvise rapidly, in the way of folk minstrels in other oral poetic traditions. For instance, the phrase *theod-cyningas* ("people-kings," "kings of the nation") is often used in place of mere *cyningas* because it fills up a half-line exactly, not because of a necessary distinction from other kinds of kings. As is pointed out by F. P. Magoun,[2] the earliest investigator of this important class of devices in Old English, metrically similar variations of *theod-cyningas* are often improvised, for the same reason: *cyninga* may be prefixed by *eorth-* ("earth-kings"), *heah-* ("high kings"), *sae-* ("sea-kings"), and other expressions.

Undoubtedly some of the Old English poems that have come down to us were composed by persons who were not in the first place *scops*, but men of the church, or at least men who had received a religious education. No doubt they sometimes wrote down their poems instead of reciting them, but they continued to use the traditional style, the formulae, and the versification of the originally unlettered, speaking or chanting, professional bards. We are not sure to what class the *Beowulf* poet belonged, but it is almost inconceivable that he was not literate, in fact well educated. He may, for instance, have borrowed some of his descriptive matter from Vergil's *Aeneid*, although of this we are not at all sure. Since *Beowulf* is so sophisticated and integrated a poem, there is a tendency to believe that it was composed, so to speak, in writing. Undoubtedly, however, most of those who knew it in Old English times heard it rather than read it.

What all this means for style is that, however liter-

---

[2] "The Oral-Formulaic Character of Anglo-Saxon Narrative Poetry," republished in *An Anthology of Beowulf Criticism*, ed. L. E. Nicholson (University of Notre Dame Press, 1963), p. 198.

ate its author was, we must think of his words as intended for the ear, not the eye. In the poem repetition reinforces the understanding, and habitual phrases and epithets are part of the tradition. Perhaps the chief qualities of his style are dignity, amplitude, and lyricism. He, and all in his tradition, understood the distance and otherness that the lofty phrase lends to events. A just appreciation of the solemnity and importance of epic happenings is implicit in the treasured repetitions of his style. He is not being tiresome, but is communicating to an audience the heroic grandeur of his subject when he says in three different ways that Beowulf killed the dragon, or even that Hrothgar went to bed. These acts are noble. They are not like ours. Each dignified reiteration of the event can be received with something like a thrill of pleasure if one realizes the choiceness of the precious subject. Thus the dignity and the amplitude.

Because *Beowulf* is so much a poem of directed emotion, and so little, comparatively, of direct narrative, its style must also be lyrical. The readjustment of the mood by the addition of an extra epithet, and then yet another, the illumination provided by repetitions with slightly different wording, the long passages of lament or of expatiation on the particular grisliness of fen, moor, or water, hardly differ, to the layman's eye, from those in Old English lyrics like *The Seafarer* and *The Wanderer*: both are mood-poetry, atmospheric; and an experiencing of the gloomy word-painting of *Beowulf* is one of the greatest and most virile pleasures of reading the poem in the original. One would wish to say, if the phrase had not been cheapened, that the composition of *Beowulf* is musical rather than narrative—more like an organ being played than a series of events being told.

As in other Germanic poetry, the style of *Beowulf* is figurative. The *kenning*, a metaphorical device described for us by the medieval Icelander Snorri Sturluson, is fairly frequent: "swan-road" and "gannet-bath" are the sea; "sea-garment" is a sail. Most often these are habitual, not freely invented. They are generally so devious that to preserve them and to make sense to a modern reader are mutually incompatible aims in a translation. There are various allied expressions, all of them part of an honorific and exalted vocabulary of the kind that is common to epic narrative everywhere. "Unlock one's word-hoard" ("say"), the patronymic epithet, like "son of Ecgtheow" ("Beowulf"), and references to the raven of battle and the eagle and the wolf who devour the slain are all to be found in *Brunanburh* and *Judith* as well as *Beowulf*. Nearly the same expressions occur frequently in other Old English poems, but they are never used more appositely than by the *Beowulf* poet. It is very difficult for us, who find these expressions extremely picturesque, to divine how habitual or how striking they seemed originally in context.

Another frequent device in *Beowulf* and in other Old English poetry is understatement or negative affirmation—meiosis or litotes—which produces controlled and usually macabre humorous effect, as when one says after falling over a cliff that it was not on that occasion that one had felt true pleasure. Much of *Brunanburh* is a tissue of such figures. Something analogous in the way of subdued, savage irony emerges from such an habitual figure as that describing one party's reaction to the fact that Wiglaf's spirit and his sword did not weaken when he helped Beowulf in the final battle with the dragon: "The serpent found this out when they had met together." The reader needs to watch out for such expressions, because they are easy to glide over.

Christianity and Paganism

It has already been suggested that the *Beowulf* poet's Christian milieu influenced his choice of supernaturally evil figures rather than men as Beowulf's enemies (although of course these figures belonged originally to the realm of folklore). In addition, however, there are a number of plainly Christian references in the body of the poem: to an Almighty who is just, to a shepherd who cares for souls and a malicious being who attacks them when they are not vigilant, to a power that helps those who help themselves. There are also definite Biblical reminiscences. Grendel is said to be descended from Cain; the sword hilt which Beowulf brings back to Hrothgar from the underwater battle with Grendel's mother has an inscription referring to an ancient race of giants, alien to God and flood-whelmed, reminiscent of the *Nephilim* or giants of Genesis vi. On the other hand, the frequent references to an inscrutable, all-controlling fate; to being fated, i.e., doomed to die; and to a man's fame as the only thing that will live after him are all in accord with what we know of Germanic pagan habits of thought, although there are no references to the ancient Germanic divinities.

It has been suggested that all or some of the "Christian" references are simply a confused amalgam of imperfectly understood Christianity and residual paganism. Our understanding of this matter has not yet reached a clear consensus, but, among other explanations, it can be said that a notion of an agency (loosely, fate or fortune) that, under the ultimate control of the Godhead, yet seems to us to control our lives inscrutably and arbitrarily, is not alien to the most sophisticated Christian thinking; consequently the *Beowulf* poet's similar references may be totally in accord with Christian principles. As far as fame is concerned, it is easy to show that poets even of the time of Shakespeare some-times made use of the idea of an "eternity of fame" as though after death a man's reputation was the most important residuum. We all now believe, as well, that certain other works around our poet's time avoided all references to Christianity and yet were written by Christians in accordance with Christian notions. *The Consolation of Philosophy* (sixth century) is the chief example.

In fact, a reading of other Old English poems may lead to the conviction that the question about whether the Christian references in *Beowulf* are, or are not, later interpolations is not a real one. What might seem to be discrete Christian elements and remnants of pagan thinking appear together in *Deor, The Dream of the Rood,* and *Maldon* and plainly come from the mind of a single author in each case. They are perhaps better described as elements of the Anglo-Saxon Christian viewpoint, which assimilated older views rather than completely discarding them.

Other Considerations

Many matters in *Beowulf* have a fairly sure historical basis. Hygelac's battle in Frisian territory occurred about A.D. 521. The Danes, Swedes, and Geats of the time are known to history. Hrothgar and Hrothulf are discussed in a twelfth-century chronicle. The site of Heorot has been located fairly reliably in a village near Roskilde, on the same island as Copenhagen. The burial mounds of Ongentheow and Ohthere in Sweden are known.

Legendary references or parallels to matters that come up in *Beowulf* exist in fair number in the Old English poems *Widsith* and *Deor,* in sagas (particularly *The Saga of Hrolf Kraki* and *The Saga of Grettir*), and elsewhere. Surprisingly, no references to a hero named Beowulf have come down to us, except for the poem itself.

The probable date and place of composition have already been touched on. If the praise that the poet gives to one Offa as the husband of Modthryth (p. 51) could be shown to be a compliment to Offa's descendant of the same name who was a famous Mercian king of the later eighth century, we should have a plausible reason for believing that *Beowulf* was written at the latter's court and in his time. Believing in an eighth-century origin, most specialists of the subject have found reason in the linguistic evidence of the apparently tenth-century manuscript to suggest that a long line of copyists, speaking different dialects, had intervened successively between it and the original composition. But recent studies have called this evidence into doubt. We now know only that the original *Beowulf* falls in the eighth, ninth, or tenth century.

The most startling archaeological find in England in recent times is the Sutton Hoo ship, found in Suffolk, near Ipswich, in 1939. In the seventh century it had been lowered into an excavation, had been partly filled with treasure, and had been covered with a mound, probably in connection with the funeral ceremonies of a king. The objects found there come up fully to the standard suggested by Scyld Scefing's funeral ship, and are of a sumptuousness and technical excellence not previously dreamed of as possible in Anglo-Saxon times. Of particular interest to readers of *Beowulf* are an ornate helmet; a sword with a remarkable inlaid pommel; a great gold buckle of intricate design; many pieces of cloisonné work in gold and garnet with spectacular patterns of great precision; the remains of a shield having among other inlays a magnificent gold dragon; a harp; and what appears to be a battle standard. Many other things were found in the ship, some suggesting a cosmopolitan culture: a great silver dish comes from the eastern Mediterranean. Like the manuscript of the poem, all these objects are housed in the British Museum in London. They are well worth seeing.

A. KENT HIEATT

BEOWULF

PROLOGUE: The Founding of the Scylding Dynasty

Indeed, we have heard of the glory of the great Danish kings in days of old and the noble deeds of the princes. Scyld Scefing[1] often drove troops of enemies from their mead-hall seats; he terrified the lords of many tribes, although he had once been a destitute foundling. He found consolation for that: he prospered under the heavens, and grew in glory, until every one of his neighbors over the sea had to obey him and pay tribute. That was a good king.

Then a son was born to him, a child in the house, sent by God to help the people—he saw the distress they had suffered before when they were without a ruler for a long time. Therefore the Lord of life, Ruler of heaven, granted worldly honor to the son of Scyld. Beowulf[2] was famous; his renown spread far and wide in the land of the Danes. A young man should do as he did, and with splendid gifts from his father's store win loyal companions who will stand by him in old age and

[1]Mythical ancestor of the Danish kings. His mysterious arrival and equally mysterious "passing" suggest divine origin; his name suggests both his function as king (shield—protector of the people), and, possibly, a nature myth ("son of a sheaf," or "child with a sheaf").

[2](I) Danish king, son of Scyld Scefing and grandfather of Hrothgar; not to be confused with Beowulf (II), hero of the poem—who is not even related to the Danish royal house.

serve the people when war comes. He who does praise-worthy deeds will prosper everywhere.

Scyld departed from him at the fated time: the mighty man went into the keeping of the Lord. His own dear retainers bore away the beloved king, who had governed them so long, to the current of the sea, as he himself had ordered while he could still use words. There in the harbor stood a ring-prowed ship, covered with ice and ready to set out; it was a craft fit for a prince. They laid their dear lord, the giver of rings, in the bosom of the ship; they put the glorious one by the mast. Many treasures and precious things from far away were brought there—never was a ship more beautifully equipped with armor and weapons of war, swords and coats of mail. On the dead lord's bosom lay a multitude of treasures that were to go far with him in the power of the flood; nor did they give him less valuable treasure than did those who first sent him forth, alone over the waves, when he was a child. They set a golden banner high over his head; then they gave him to the sea and let the water carry him away. Their spirits were saddened, their hearts mournful. Men on earth, even the wisest of counselors, do not know how to tell who truly received that cargo.

PART I: The Cleansing of Heorot

Heorot Is Built and Assaulted by the Monster Grendel

1

When the prince his father was gone, Beowulf, son of Scyld, reigned over the people; he was renowned among nations for a long time. To him in turn was born high Healfdene, who ruled the Danes gloriously as long as he lived—a venerable leader, fierce in battle. To Healfdene, the leader of hosts, four children all told were born into the world: Heorogar and Hrothgar and Halga the Good, and a daughter, who, they say, was Onela's[3] queen—consort of the Swedish king.

Then Hrothgar was granted success in battle and glory in war, so that his friends and kinsmen obeyed him willingly, and his band of warriors grew large. It came into his mind to order a great mead-hall built, one which the children of men should hear of forever; there he would give out all that God gave him (except the public land and the lives of men) to young and old. I have heard that he then ordered work to adorn the building from nations far and wide throughout this earth. The time soon came when the greatest of halls was quite ready, and the ruler whose word was widely respected gave it the name of Heorot. He did not forget his promise to give out rings and treasures at the feast. The hall towered, high and wide-gabled: it awaited the hostile flames of hateful fire. The time had not yet come when deadly hate would arise between a son and father-in-law after a deed of violence.

This was a time of suffering for the powerful demon who dwelt in darkness, when he heard loud rejoicing in the hall every day. There was the sound of the harp and the sweet song of the minstrel, who told about the creation of men, long ago; he said that the Almighty made the earth, the beautiful land bounded by the water; then, triumphant, he placed the sun and the moon as a light to lighten those who dwell on the land, and adorned the earth with branches and leaves; and he also created every living creature which moves after its kind. —Thus the retainers of Hrothgar lived in joy and happiness, until the hellish fiend began his wicked deeds.

---

[3]King of Sweden (see genealogical tables), who killed Heardred, king of the Geats, and was later killed by his rebellious nephew Eadgils.

This grim spirit was called Grendel. A notorious prowler of the waste lands, he held sway in the moors, the fen and fastness. The miserable creature had long inhabited the haunts of monsters, since the Creator had condemned him and all his race, the progeny of Cain,[4] in vengeance for the slaying of Abel. Cain got no joy by his murderous act, but was banished by the eternal Lord; God drove him from mankind for that crime. Of his race were born all evil broods—ogres, elves, and monsters, and the giants who contended against God for a long time—he paid them back for that!

2

When night fell, Grendel went to seek out the lofty house, to see how the Danes had settled down after drinking beer. There, inside, he found the band of noble warriors, sleeping after the feast: they did not know sorrow and the misery of men. Grim and greedy, the evil creature was alert at once: the cruel and savage monster took from their beds thirty of the thanes. Then he left there, exulting in his booty, seeking out his home with his fill of slaughter.

Then at dawn, with the break of day, Grendel's might in warfare was no secret to men. Where there had been feast and merrymaking, weeping arose, a great cry in the morning.

The glorious chief sat joyless; the prince, mighty of old, endured sorrow for his thanes when they saw the track of the foe, the accursed demon. The trouble now was severe beyond measure, hateful and long lasting: there was no further respite, but again the next night he committed more murder—he did not shrink from hostile act and wicked deed, for he was too fixed in the

---

[4]The Biblical first murderer; see Genesis 4: 1–15.

fetters of sin. Now it was easy to find a man who looked
for a resting place further away, a bed in other build-
ings, when he had seen clear signs of the hall-visitor's
hatred: he who escaped the enemy kept himself fur-
ther away in a safer place.

The monster prevailed in this way and contended
against right, one against all, until the best of houses
stood empty. That lasted a long time: for twelve win-
ters the Danish lord was afflicted with these troubles
and suffered great sorrow. Sad lays made it openly
known to men that Grendel warred against Hrothgar
for a long time; he waged warfare, committed wicked
deeds and hostile acts, for many seasons of continual
strife. He did not want peace with any of the Danish
host; he did not wish to stop his deadly evil, nor to
settle the feud with payment—none of the counselors
had reason to expect great compensation from the hand
of the murderer. On the contrary, the dark death-shadow
persecuted young and old, lingered and ambushed. He
held the misty moors in perpetual darkness—no man
knows where such demons go.

Thus the enemy of mankind, the fearful outcast,
often did many wicked deeds and perpetrated greivous
injuries. In the dark nights he prowled Heorot, the richly
decorated hall; but he could not approach the throne,
the seat where treasure was given—God prevented
him—nor feel gratitude for gifts.

That was heartbreaking misery for the Scylding's
lord. Many great leaders frequently sat in counsel pon-
dering plans, in deliberation as to what would be best
for brave-spirited men to do against the awful horror.
At times they made sacrifices to idols in heathen tem-
ples, entreating the devil to help them relieve the dis-
tress of the people. Such was their custom, the hope of
heathens—their thoughts were on hell, for they did not
know their Creator, the Judge of deeds: they neither
knew the Lord God nor understood how to worship

the Protector of the heavens, the Ruler of glories. Woe
to him who, in cruel affliction, shall thrust his soul into
the embrace of the fire—he shall know no comfort or
change. Well shall it be for him who may go to the
Lord after the day of death and ask for peace in the
bosom of the Father!

Beowulf's Arrival

3

So Healfdene's son brooded continually over the
trouble of the time; nor could the wise prince turn that
misery aside. The strife which had come upon the peo-
ple was too hateful and enduring, a cruel, dire distress—
the greatest of evils that come by night.

A brave man of the tribe of the Geats, a thane of
Hygelac,[5] heard in his homeland of Grendel's deeds.
He was the strongest and mightiest man alive, noble
and stalwart. He ordered a good ship prepared for
him, saying he wished to seek out the warrior king over
the road of the swans, since that glorious leader had
need of men. Wise men did not blame him for this
venture, although he was dear to them: they encour-
aged the brave man, and looked at the omens. The
hero had chosen the keenest champions he could find
among the Geatish people, and it was as one of fifteen
that he led the way to the ship, a skilled seaman guid-
ing his band along the shore.

In good time the boat was on the waves, floating
under the cliffs. Watchful men climbed the prow. The
ocean streams eddied, sea washed against sand, as the
men bore bright trappings and splendid armor into the
ship. The men shoved out: the warriors launched the
well-braced craft on the longed-for journey. Driven by

---

[5]Beowulf's uncle, king of the Geats (a tribe living in southern Sweden).

the wind, the boat went over the billowy sea, foamy
necked, like a bird, until in due time on the following
day the curved prow had advanced so that the seafar-
ers saw land; they sighted the shining sea cliffs, the
steep banks of the shore, the broad headlands. The sea
had been crossed and the voyage was at an end. Quickly
the people of the Geats mounted on the land and
moored the ship—their battle garments, shirts of mail,
rattled—and thanked God that their voyage had been
easy.

From the wall the Danish guard, who had the duty
of keeping watch on the sea cliffs, saw bright shields
and ready armor brought over the gangway: he was
very curious to know what men these were. Hrothgar's
thane rode his horse to the shore, brandishing a mighty
spear in his hand, and spoke in formal words: "What
manner of men are you, warriors in armor, who have
thus come in your lofty ship here across the sea? I have
been coast guard here for a long time, holding watch
by the sea so that no enemy force might harry the land
of the Danes. Never have armed men come here more
openly—yet you did not have leave from our warriors,
or the agreement of kinsmen. Never have I seen a
mightier nobleman in the world, a greater man in armor,
than one among you: surely that is no mere hall re-
tainer exalted with weapons—may his splendid counte-
nance, his peerless appearance, never belie him! —Now
I must know your lineage before you may go further,
possibly spying on the land of the Danes; strangers,
seafarers, now hear my plain thought: best make it
known quickly where you come from."

4

The chief answered him; the leader of the band
said, "We are people of the Geatish nation, Hygelac's
hearth companions. My father was a noble leader well

9

known among nations; he was called Ecgtheow. He lived through many winters, and was an old man when he departed from this world. Wise men remember him well all over the earth. We come with friendly intentions to seek your lord, the son of Healfdene; be of good counsel to us! We have a weighty errand to the glorious lord of the Danes—nor, I think, will there be anything secret about it. You know whether what we have heard is true: that an enemy—I know not who, a mysterious persecutor—shows his strange hostility among the Danes in the dark nights and works injury and slaughter in a terrible way. I may be able to give Hrothgar sincere good counsel as to how he, who is so good and wise, may overcome the fiend—if a change is ever to be, if a cure for these miserable afflictions is to come in its turn, and sorrows end. Otherwise, he will suffer trials and distress for ever after, as long as the best of houses remains in its lofty place."

The guard, a fearless officer, spoke as he sat there on his horse: "An acute warrior who has a clear mind should be a judge of both words and deeds. I understand that this band is friendly to the lord of the Danes. Go on with your weapons and armor; I will guide you. Also, I shall bid my men to guard your boat honorably against every enemy, watch over the newly tarred vessel on the sand, until the curved-prowed ship again bears its beloved lord over the sea to the land of the Geats. One who does brave deeds will be allowed to survive the storm of battle unhurt."

They went on their way. The ship remained; the spacious vessel was moored with a rope, fast at anchor. Over the warriors' cheek-guards shone boar figures, decorated with gold, shining and hardened by fire: the warlike boar kept guard over the fierce ones. The company hastened until they could perceive the timbered hall, splendid and decorated with gold; that was the most famous building under heaven, the dwelling of the mighty lord; its light shone over many lands. The guard showed them that bright home of brave men so that they could go straight to it, then turned his horse and said, "It is time for me to go. May the almighty Father, by his grace, keep you safe in your undertaking! I shall go to the sea to keep watch against hostile bands."

5

The street was paved with stone, and the path guided the band of men. Chain-mail gleamed and bright iron rings sang in their armor as they came to the hall in their warlike gear. Weary of the sea, they set their broad, strong shields against the wall of the building and sat down on the bench, with a ringing of chain mail. Their spears, war gear of seamen, stood gathered together, the ashwood gleaming gray at the tip; the band was well equipped with weapons.

There a noble champion asked the warriors of their descent: "From where have you brought decorated shields, gray coats of mail and visored helmets, a host of spears? I am Hrothgar's herald and officer. Never have I seen a bolder band of strangers. I think you have come to Hrothgar in daring mood: not as exiles seeking refuge, but as brave men in search of glory."

The famous hero answered him: strong in his helmet, the valiant Geat replied, "We are Hygelac's table-companions: Beowulf is my name. I wish to tell my errand to the son of Healfdene, the glorious prince who is your lord, if he who is so great will allow us to greet him."

Wulfgar replied (he was a prince of the Wendels,[6]

---

[6]Possibly the Vandels; very likely, the inhabitants of Vendel, in Sweden, or Vendill, in Jutland.

well known for his wisdom and valor): "I will ask the lord and ruler of the Danes, the giver of rings, as you request. I shall tell the glorious lord of your venture and quickly bring you back the answer the great one thinks fit to give me."

Quickly he turned to the place where Hrothgar, old and gray, sat with his band of nobles; the valiant warrior went up and stood by the shoulder of the Danish lord—he knew the custom of the court. Wulfgar spoke to his lord: "Geatish people are here, come from over the expanse of the water; the warriors call their chief Beowulf. My lord, they ask to exchange words with you. Do not refuse them your answer, gracious Hrothgar! They are well-armed men who seem worthy of the respect of nobles; and the chief who led these warriors here is certainly a powerful man."

6

Hrothgar, the Scyldings' protector, spoke: "I knew him when he was a boy. His father was called Ecgtheow: to him Hrethel,[7] king of the Geats, gave his only daughter in marriage. Now his brave son has come here to see a loyal friend. Seafarers who have carried gifts for the pleasure of the Geats said that this famous warrior has the strength of thirty men in his grip. I expect that holy God in his grace has sent him to the Danes to help us against Grendel's terror. I shall offer the hero treasures for his daring. Hurry: bid the band of kinsmen to come in to see me and tell them that the Danish people welcome them."

Wulfgar went to the door and brought his message from within: "My victorious lord, the ruler of Denmark, bids me say to you that he knows of your noble descent, and that you courageous men from over the

---

[7]Father of Hygelac and grandfather of Beowulf (see genealogical tables).

sea are welcome to him. Now go in your battle gear, wearing your helmets, to see Hrothgar; let the shields and wooden spears remain here to await the result of the conference."

The hero arose with many a warrior around him: a troop of mighty thanes. Some stayed there to guard the war gear, as their leader ordered them, while the others hastened under Heorot's roof, the herald guiding them. The helmeted leader went on until he stood on the hearth.

His mail, the battle net linked by the skill of the smith, shone as Beowulf spoke: "Hail, Hrothgar! I am Hygelac's kinsman and retainer, and I have undertaken many a glorious deed in my youth. In my native land I heard of Grendel's doings. Seafarers say that this hall, the best of buildings, stands idle and useless to all when the evening light fades under heaven's vault.

"The noblest and wisest counselors of my people advised me to come to you, lord Hrothgar, because they knew of my great strength. They themselves saw me when, stained with the blood of enemies, I came from battles, when I bound five giants and destroyed their race, and killed water monsters on the waves at night; I endured great hardship to avenge their persecution of the Geats—they had asked for trouble! I ground down those fierce creatures, and now I will fight against the monster Grendel; alone I shall settle the dispute with the demon.

"Chief of the Danes, protector of the nation, I want to ask one boon of you now—do not refuse me, defender of warriors and friend of the people, now that I have come so far—that I alone, with my bold troop of nobles, may purge Heorot.

"Also, I have learned that the monster, in his recklessness, does not care to use weapons; then, so that Hygelac, my lord, may rejoice over me in his heart, I will scorn to bear a sword or broad shield to the battle but will grapple against the fiend with my hands and fight for my life, enemy against enemy; he whom death takes there must trust to the judgment of the Lord. I expect that if he can have his way, he will devour the Geatish people in the war-hall without hesitation—as he has often done to mighty warriors.

"If death takes me, there will be no need for you to cover my head, for Grendel will have my bloodstained body; he will bear off the bloody corpse to devour it. The solitary monster will eat ruthlessly, staining his moor retreat—and you will not have to worry longer over the disposal of my body. If I fall in battle, send Hygelac this best of war garments, finest of mail, which protects my breast; it is an heirloom of Hrethel, the work of Weland[8] the smith. Destiny always comes about as it must!"

7

Hrothgar, defender of the Scyldings, spoke: "You have come to help us and fight in our defence, my friend Beowulf. Your father's blows brought about a great feud when he killed Heatholaf, among the Wyflings, so that his people, fearing war would result, could not shelter him. From there he sought out the Danish people over the rolling waves, visiting the Scyldings at the time when I first reigned over Denmark and held the gracious realm, treasure city of warriors, in my youth. Heorogar was dead then—my elder brother was no longer living; he was a better man than I! After that I settled the feud with money. I sent ancient treasure over the water to the Wylfings; in return, Ecgtheow swore oaths to me.

"It is with great sorrow in my heart that I tell any

---

[8]A legendary Germanic smith; his name was a guarantee of excellent workmanship.

man what Grendel has done to me in his malice—what
injuries and calamities he has brought about in Heorot.
My troop of retainers has grown smaller; destiny has
swept my warriors off with Grendel's terror. God can
easily put an end to the deeds of the mad ravager!
Often warriors drunk with beer have vowed over the
ale cup to wait in the beer hall with their swords for
Grendel's onslaught. Then in the morning, when day
broke, this mead-hall was bloodstained; all the bench
planks were soaked with blood, the hall stained with
battle gore. I had the fewer loyal men, beloved veteran
retainers, since death had carried them off.

"—Now sit down to the feast, and, in due time,
listen to lays of warriors' victories, as your heart may
prompt you."

A bench in the beer hall was yielded to the men of
the Geats, and the brave champions went to sit there. A
servant did his duty; bearing a decorated ale cup in his
hands, he poured out the bright drink. From time to
time a clear-voiced minstrel sang in Heorot, and the
large company of warriors, Danes and Geats, rejoiced
together.

Beowulf Meets a Challenge From Unferth

8

Then Unferth, son of Ecglaf, spoke: sitting at the
feet of the Scylding lord, he burst out in hostile words.
The expedition of Beowulf, the brave seafarer, was
most displeasing to him, for he did not want any other
man on earth to win more glory in the world than he
himself. "Are you that Beowulf who contested against
Breca swimming on the wide sea, where you two in
your pride dared the deep waters and ventured your
lives because of foolish boasting? No one, neither friend
nor enemy, could dissuade you two from that sorry

undertaking when you swam in the sea; there you embraced the ocean stream, traveled over the paths of the sea with swinging hands, glided over the water. The ocean swelled in waves, in a winter flood.

"You both labored seven nights in the power of the water, but he had more might, and surpassed you in swimming. Then in the morning the sea carried him up on Norwegian land; from there he sought his own native country, the dear land of the Brondings, and there he governed the people, stronghold, and treasure. Indeed, the son of Beanstan carried out his boast against you. Therefore, although you have always proved strong in the storm of battle, in grim war, I expect the worse results from you if you dare to wait for Grendel all night long."

Beowulf, Ecgtheow's son, said in answer, "Well, my friend Unferth, drunk with beer, you have said a great many things about Breca and described his venture. I say this is the truth: that I had more strength in the sea, in struggling with the waves, than any other man. We two, being young men still in the time of early youth, agreed and vowed that we would hazard our lives out on the sea, and we carried it out in this way.

"When we swam in the sea we each had a naked sword firmly in hand to defend ourselves against whales. He could not outdistance me, swimming more quickly in the sea, nor did I have any desire to go far from him. Thus we were together in the water for a period of five nights, until the flood drove us apart: the waters were welling, the weather most cold, and night darkening, and the north wind, grim as battle, turned against us; the waves were rough.

"The temper of the sea fishes was aroused. There my body armor, hard and strongly linked together, gave me help—the woven battle mail decorated with gold lay on my breast. A hostile, deadly foe drew me to the bottom: the grim creature had me fast in his grip;

16

however, it was granted to me to pierce the monster with the point of my battle sword. The mighty sea beast was dispatched by my hand in the storm of battle.

9

"Thus the oppressors harassed me constantly. I dealt with them with my good sword as they deserved— nor did the wicked destroyers of men have the pleasure of feasting on me, sitting around the banquet at the bottom of the sea. In the morning, they lay upon the shore wounded by the sword, put to sleep by the blade so that they could never afterward hinder seafarers from making their way over the high seas. Light came from the east, God's bright beacon, and the water subsided, so that I could see the headlands of the sea, the windy walls. Destiny often helps the undoomed man, when his valor avails him! Thus it was my lot to slay nine sea monsters with the sword. I have never heard of a harder battle fought by night under the vault of heaven, nor of a man more distressed in the ocean; yet I survived that hostile grasp alive, though weary from the undertaking. Then the sea bore me off along the current of the flood; the welling water brought me onto the land of the Lapps.

"I have never heard any such perilous exploit told of you. Never yet did Breca, or you either, do such a bold deed in battle with your shining swords (although I do not think that one of my greater exploits), although you killed your brothers, your own close relatives; for that you will endure damnation in hell, no matter how clever you may be.

"I tell you the truth, son of Ecglaf: Grendel, that terrible monster, would never have done so many outrages in Heorot, such damage to your lord, if your heart and spirit were as warlike as you yourself say; he has discovered that he need not much dread the enmity of your people, the blades of the victorious Danes, so he takes his toll and shows mercy to none of the Danish nation, but enjoys himself, kills and dispatches, and does not expect battle from the Danes. But now I will soon show him the Geats' strength and courage in war. After that, whoever can do so will go boldly to the mead-hall when the morning light of another day, the sun clothed in radiance, shines from the south over the sons of men."

The generous king, gray haired and famous in battle, rejoiced at this. The prince of the glorious Danes expected help: the guardian of the people saw in Beowulf a mind firmly resolved.

Then there was much laughter of men, the pleasing sound of music and joyous words. Wealhtheow, Hrothgar's queen, came forward courteously; adorned with gold, she greeted the men in the hall. The noble wife first gave the cup to the Danish lord, bidding him to be blithe at the beer drinking, and the famous king gladly took his share of the feast and the cup. Then the Helming[9] lady went around to each group of retainers, young and old, giving the precious cups, until the time came when the astute queen, adorned with rings, bore the mead cup to Beowulf. She greeted the leader of the Geats and thanked God in well-chosen words that her wish had come about, that she might expect from any man relief from attacks.

The fierce warrior received the cup from Wealhtheow, and, ready for battle, he said: "When I set out on the sea and embarked in that boat with my band of men, I resolved that I would certainly do the will of your people—or else fall in the field of battle, fast in the grip of the foe. I shall do great deeds of valor, or else meet my life's end in this mead-hall!"

These words, the vow of the Geat, pleased the lady

---

[9]Wealhtheow's family.

well. The noble, ring-adorned queen went to sit by her
lord. Once again, as before, mighty words were spoken
in the hall, songs of the victorious people, and the
retainers were happy. Presently the son of Healfdene
wished to go to his evening rest: he knew an attack on
the high hall had been planned by the monster from
the time when they first saw the light of the sun until
the darkening night with dusky shades came moving
over all, black under the clouds.

All the band arose. Hrothgar saluted Beowulf and
wished him good fortune and control of the wine hall,
saying, "Never before, while I could lift hand and shield,
have I given over the splendid hall of the Danes to any
man, until now to you. Now guard and keep the best of
houses; consider your glory, show your mighty valor,
and watch against the enemy. You shall not lack for
good things if you survive this valorous work with your
life."

The Fight With Grendel

10

Then Hrothgar left them; the Danish prince went
out of the hall with his band of warriors. The chieftain
wished to seek his bedfellow, Wealhtheow, the queen.
The King of glory had, men said, set a guard against
Grendel—one who performed a special service for the
lord of the Danes and offered a watch against the
giant. Indeed, the chief of the Geats eagerly trusted in
his own courage and might, and the grace of the Creator.

Now Beowulf took off his iron mail and the helmet
from his head. He gave his adorned sword, the most
choice of steel weapons, to an attendant, and ordered
him to guard the battle gear. Before he climbed into
bed the brave Geat spoke this vow: "I do not consider
myself a lesser fighter than Grendel does himself; there-

fore I will not kill him with a sword, and deprive him
of life in that way—though I surely could. He does not
know the proper ways to strike back at me and hew my
shield, although he is renowned for hostile works. No:
this night we two will abstain from swords, if he dares
seek out a fight without weapon. Afterwards, may the
wise God, the holy Lord, assign glory to whichever side
seems fitting to him."

Then the brave warrior lay down; his pillow re-
ceived the hero's face, and around him many a bold
seaman lay down on his bed in the hall. None of them
thought that he would ever hereafter return to his
beloved home, or see his people or the noble dwelling
where he grew up, for they had heard that in the past
murderous death had borne off all too many of the
Danish people. But the Lord granted the destiny of
success in war to the Geatish people; he gave them such
comfort and help that they overcame their enemy,
through the power and might of one man. It is truly
said that mighty God has always ruled mankind.

In the dark night the one who walked in shadow
came gliding. The warriors who were to guard that
gabled house slept—all but one. Men knew that if God
did not wish it, the demon foe could not draw them
down into the shades. But one watched against the foe
in deadly rage, and angrily awaited the outcome of the
battle.

11

Then, from the moor, Grendel came moving under
the misty hills. God's curse rested on him. The foe of
men intended to ensnare some human being in the
high hall. He advanced under the clouds to a place
where he could easily recognize the wine hall of men,
decorated with gold. That was not the first time he had
visited Hrothgar's home—but never in all the days of

his life, before or after, did he find thanes in the hall with worse results for himself! The joyless creature came to the building.

The door, fastened with forged bands, gave way at once when he touched it with his hands. Then the evil-minded creature, in his rage, tore open the entrance to the building and quickly trod on the handsome paved floor. The fiend's temper was aroused; from his eyes came an unlovely light, like a hellish flame. He saw in the building many warriors—the band of kinsmen sleeping together, a troop of young warriors—and his spirit exulted. The horrible monster intended to tear the life from the body of every one of them before day came. He hoped for his fill of feasting. But it was not destined that he would be able to partake of any more of mankind after that night.

Hygelac's mighty nephew watched to see how the evildoer would carry out his attack. Nor did the monster intend to delay, but swiftly grasped, in his first gesture, a sleeping warrior: he tore him up furiously, bit into muscles and drank the blood in streams, swallowed huge morsels, and quickly consumed the entire corpse, even feet and hands. He moved along further and reached toward the hero where he lay in his bed. The fiend grasped at Beowulf, who saw his hostile plan at once and sat up, pitting his weight against the monster's arm.

Now the ghoul found that never in the world, anywhere on earth, had he met a man with a mightier handgrip. He became afraid in his heart, but he could not get away any the sooner. He was eager to be off; he wanted to flee to his hiding place and seek out the company of devils—his circumstances there were unlike any he had ever before encountered in all the days of his life. The brave kinsman of Hygelac remembered his vows of that evening: he stood upright and got a fast hold on the monster; fingers were bursting as the giant tried to turn away, but the hero stepped further. However he could manage it, the infamous wretch meant to take flight to some place further away—to flee to his retreat in the fens; he knew the strength of his fingers was in a fierce grip. That journey to Heorot was a sorry one for the enemy! The mead-hall resounded so with the din that it brought terror to the Danes in their stronghold and alarmed all the brave warriors.

Both the fierce claimants to the building were enraged, and the hall resounded. It was a great wonder that the wine hall withstood the clash of the warriors, that the fair building did not fall to the ground; but it was firmly fastened in a skillful way, both inside and out, with iron bands. They say that many a mead-bench adorned with gold started from the floor where the angry foes struggled. Before that night no Dane had thought that any man could ever break up that excellent hall, adorned with antlers, by any means at all; they thought none had the skill to pull it asunder—unless it should be swallowed by flames, in the embrace of the fire.

Strange noise rose up again and again; a dreadful terror stirred the Danes and seized every man who heard through the wall the lamentation of God's adversary, singing his terrible dirge, his song of the defeat—the captive of hell wailing sorely, for he who was strongest and mightiest of living men held him fast.

12

The last thing the chief of heroes wished was to let the murderous intruder go alive; he did not consider Grendel's life to be useful to anyone. Now Beowulf's noble companions were drawing their ancient swords, wishing to defend the life of the lord, their glorious leader, in any way they could. The stouthearted warriors engaged in combat and tried to hew at the monster from every side, seeking his life, but what they did not know was that no sword could touch the evildoer, not even the choicest steel on earth: for he had cast a spell which made weapons useless, every blade!

But he was to make a miserable parting from life on that day; the alien spirit was destined to travel afar in the power of fiends. Now he who had afflicted the hearts of mankind so much in earlier days and had committed so many crimes—he was at odds with God—discovered that his body was of no use to him, for Hygelac's brave kinsman had him in his grip.

Neither could bear to see the other stay alive. The horrible monster felt mortal pain as a huge wound tore apart his shoulder: his sinews sprang open and muscle ripped from bone. Glory in battle was granted to Beowulf; Grendel had to flee away, mortally wounded, down into the fen to seek his joyless dwelling. He knew all too well that his life had come to its end, that the number of his days had run out. The wish of all the Danes had come to pass after the bloody conflict.

That wise, brave man who had come from far away had purged Hrothgar's hall and saved it from evil. He rejoiced in the night's work, in his deeds of valor; the leader of the Geat warriors had carried out his vow to the Danes, and had so remedied all the grief and hard sorrow they had endured before, and had had to suffer out of dire necessity—no little affliction. A sign of victory was manifest to all when the brave warrior put the hand, arm, and shoulder under the vaulted roof: there was Grendel's grip, all together.

Joy in Heorot

13

They say that in the morning many warriors gathered in the hall. Leaders of the people came from near and far, through distant regions, to see the marvel and gaze at the enemy's tracks. His departure from life did not seem sad to anyone who observed the vanquished creature's trail and saw how with weary spirit, overcome by strife, he made his way from there into the mere of the water demons; doomed and put to flight, he left a bloody track. Blood surged up in the sea water and the terrible turmoil of waves there was mingled with hot gore, boiling with blood from the battle. There he hid himself, doomed to death, until, deprived of all joys, he gave up his life and his heathen soul in his fen refuge: hell received him there.

From there the veterans, with many younger men too, returned from the joyful journey, boldly riding their horses from the mere. Beowulf's fame was proclaimed, and many said over and over again that north or south, between the seas and over the wide earth, there was no better warrior under the compass of the skies, nor one more worthy of power. But they did not find any fault at all with their dear lord, gracious Hrothgar, for he was a good king.

From time to time the warriors let their bay horses gallop, racing each other where the pathways were known to be good. At times, one of the king's distinguished thanes, whose mind was full of lays and who remembered many old traditions, composed a new poem, in properly linked words. Skillfully he began to treat of Beowulf's venture, and successfully he uttered an apt tale, varying his words.

He told all he had heard about Sigemund's[10] deeds of valor—many strange things about the struggles of that son of Waels, his travels far and wide, feuds and violent deeds, which the sons of men knew little about, except only Fitela: his uncle spoke of such things to his nephew when he wanted, for they were always comrades in arms at every battle and had slain a great many giants with their swords. To Sigemund came no small fame after his death-day, since the strong warrior had killed the dragon who was guardian of a treasure hoard. Under the gray stone the prince's son dared the bold deed alone—not even Fitela was with him. Yet it turned out well for him, in that his sword went through the wondrous dragon until that splendid iron weapon stood still in the wall, and the dragon was slain. The hero's valor had brought it to pass that he might enjoy the ring hoard at his own will. Sigemund loaded a boat and bore bright treasure into the bosom of the ship; the dragon melted in its own heat.

This great warrior was the most renowned of wanderers all over the world for his deeds of valor—he had met such success—after Heremod's[11] fame in war had faded, his might and valor gone. He was betrayed into the power of enemies among giants and was soon put to death. Trouble after trouble oppressed him too long: he was a mortal grief to his people and to all their princes. Many a wise man had, in times past, lamented the daring chief's journey, having expected a remedy for misfortunes from him, and hoped that the royal prince might prosper and come to be the equal of his noble father, keeping the people safe and guarding the stronghold and treasure, realm of heroes and home-

---

[10] A great legendary Germanic hero; best known to us today through a different version used by Wagner in his operas (the "ring cycle"), in which Siegmund's son, Siegfried, is the dragon-slayer.

[11] A Danish king, presumably predecessor of Scyld Scefing; regarded here as the prototype of the bad king.

land of the Danes. The kinsman of Hygelac was a joy to his people and to all mankind, whereas crime grasped Heremod.

Racing from time to time, they came along the sandy track on their horses. The morning light was hastening on. Many a valiant man went to the high wall to see the curious wonder; so too the king himself, guardian of the ring hoard, came from his wife's chambers. The glorious lord, famous for his nobility, came with a great company, and his queen also came along the mead-path with a troop of women.

14

Hrothgar went to the hall; as he stood on the flight of steps and looked at the steep golden roof and Grendel's hand, he said: "For this sight, may thanks be offered to the Almighty at once! I have endured many horrors and much grief at Grendel's hand. God, the King of glory, can always work wonder after wonder! Not long ago I did not expect ever to see a remedy for any of my woes; the best of houses stood stained with blood, gory from battle—a great sorrow to all the wise counselors. They did not think they would ever be able to protect the stronghold of the people from foes, demons, and evil spirits. Now a warrior has done the deed—through God's might—that none of us were skillful enough to accomplish before. Indeed, if the woman who bore such a son into the world still lives, she may say that the eternal Lord was gracious to her in her childbearing.

"Now, Beowulf, best of men, I will love you in my heart as my own son; keep this new kinship well from now on. You shall not lack any worldly goods that are within my power. I have often given a reward for less, and honored with treasure a lesser man, inferior in battle. You have done such deeds that your fame will live forever. May the Almighty reward you with good, as he did just now!"

Beowulf, the son of Ecgtheow, replied, "It was with good will that we did that deed of valor, undertook that fight, and boldly dared the strength of the mysterious enemy. I greatly wish that you could have seen him yourself—the fiend in all his trappings, weary to death. I intended to pin him down to his deathbed quickly with hard grasps, so that he should lie low, struggling for life because of my handgrip, unless his body should escape. I could not hinder his going, when the Lord did not wish it so; I could not hold the deadly foe firmly. The fiend was too powerful in his departure. Nevertheless he left his hand to save his life: his arm and shoulder remained behind; nor did the wretch gain any consolation. No longer shall the evildoer live, hardened in sins, for sorrow has seized him close in its forceful grip, its evil fetters. There the guilty creature must await the great judgment, and find how the glorious Lord will impose his sentence on him."

Unferth was a more silent man now; he made no boasting speeches about war deeds after the court had seen the hand hung under the high roof, the fiend's fingers put there because of the hero's prowess—the tips of those fingers, at the nails, were just like steel; the claws of the heathen fighter were hateful spikes. Everyone said that no hard weapon, not even the best of heirloom swords, could reach the bloody battle-hand of the monster to do it harm.

15

Orders were quickly given to decorate Heorot inside. Many men and women adorned that wine building with their hands. Tapestries gleaming with gold shone on the walls and there were many wonderful sights for everyone to gaze on. That splendid house, bound fast with iron bands within, was very much broken up, and the hinges were cracked apart; only the roof survived uninjured in every respect when the monster, stained with guilty deeds, turned in flight, despairing of life. It is not easy to flee death: let him try it who will, he must needs seek out the place prepared for the souls of men on earth, when his body sleeps fast in the grave after the feast of life.

Now it was the proper time for Healfdene's son to go to the hall: the king himself wished to partake of the feast. Never have I heard of a band of people who behaved themselves better or gathered in a greater number around their lord. They turned to the benches and rejoiced in the feast, and the mighty kinsmen, Hrothgar and Hrothulf,[12] courteously took many a cup of mead in the high hall. Heorot was filled with friends: there was no treachery among the Scyldings at that time.

As a reward of victory, Hrothgar gave Beowulf a golden banner, a decorated battle standard, a helmet and a coat of mail, and many men saw a glorious, precious sword brought before the warrior. Beowulf received the cup on the hall floor—he did not need to be ashamed of his rich gifts before the men! I have not heard of many men giving four golden treasures to another at the banquet more graciously. Around the top of the helmet a rim wound with wires formed a protection for the head, so that when the warrior was to go forth against his foes no sharp sword could do him injury.

Then the king ordered eight gold-bridled horses to be led onto the floor, into the enclosure; on one of them was a saddle skillfully decorated, ornamented with

---

[12]Hrothgar's nephew (see genealogical tables); we know from other sources that Wealhtheow's confidence in him was misplaced: after the death of Hrothgar, he killed at least one nephew and took the throne.

jewels. This was the war saddle of the king himself,
which Hrothgar had used when he wanted to join in
swordplay—and never did the valor of that famous
chief fail; he was always at the front when the slaugh-
tered fell. And then the ruler of the Danes gave all this
into Beowulf's keeping, horses and weapons, and bade
him enjoy them well. The glorious lord, guardian of
the treasure of heroes, paid for the combat with horses
and treasure in such a manly fashion that no man with
a regard for the truth could find fault with him.

Hrothgar's Feast

16

Beyond that he gave precious heirlooms over the
mead-bench to each of the band of nobles who came
with Beowulf on the ocean voyage, and he ordered
gold to be given for the one whom Grendel had foully
murdered before—as the monster would have done to
more of them, if God in his wisdom had not put des-
tiny and a man's courage in his way. The Creator ruled
all mankind, as he still does now—thus it is best every-
where to have understanding and forethought of mind.
He who long enjoys days of trial in this world shall
experience many things, both good and bad.

Then there was song and music before the Danish
king; the harp was touched, many a tale was told, and
Hrothgar's minstrel recited a lay to entertain them along
the mead-bench. He told of the sons of Finn,[13] of how
disaster befell them, and how the Scylding Hnaef, hero
of the Half-Danes, fell on the Frisian battlefield.

---

[13]King of the Frisians. Apparently his marriage to the Danish princess
Hildeburh was intended to settle a feud; it did not, for on a visit to Finn's
court, Hnaef, Hildeburh's brother, was killed. The Danes (under the leader-
ship of Hengest) and Frisians fought on for several days, until an uneasy truce
was arranged. The *Beowulf* poet tells us what happened after that.

Hildeburh, indeed, had small cause to praise the good faith of the giants:[14] through no fault of her own, she was bereft of dear ones, son and brother, who fell doomed in the fray, wounded by spears. That was a sad lady! It was not for nothing that Hoc's daughter mourned the decree of fate when morning came and, by daylight, she could see her kinsmen murdered. Where he had enjoyed before the greatest earthly joys, war swept away all Finn's thanes, except a very few, so that he could not at all bring the fight with Hengest to a finish in that meeting place, nor drive out the remnant with the prince's thane by battle.

But they offered him terms: that they should give them room on one of the hall floors, with a high seat, where they would control half, as against the children of the enemy; and in dealing out gifts, every day Finn, son of Folcwald, would honor the Danes, Hengest's troop, with just as great a share of rings and precious treasure decorated with gold as he gave to encourage the people of the Frisians in the beer hall. Then they swore a firm treaty of peace on both sides.

Finn made solemn vows to Hengest: that he would hold the survivors in honor according to the judgment of wise counselors; and that no man there should break the agreement by word or deed, or even complain of it in malice, although they would be following the slayer of their leader—they had to do this since they were without a lord. Then if any one of the Frisians were to recall the feud in provocative speech, the sword's edge should settle it. The oath was prepared, and gold brought from the hoard.

Hnaef, the best of the Danish warriors, was ready on the funeral pyre. At the pyre everyone could see

---

[14]"Giants" here may mean Jutes, a tribe whose name was spelled similarly to the word for "giant": or it may be either a term used for "enemies" in general or a by-name for the Frisians (compare "Scylding" for "Dane").

bloodstained mail and the golden images of boars, iron-hard on the helmets, and many a nobleman killed with wounds—no few had fallen in the slaughter. Hildeburh then ordered her own son entrusted to the heat in Hnaef's pyre, his body to be burned and put on the pyre by his uncle's shoulder. The lady lamented and uttered mournful dirges. The warrior was raised up, and the greatest of funeral pyres wound to the clouds, roared before the mounds; heads melted, and open wounds burst—blood sprang out from the grievous bodily wounds. Flame, greediest of spirits, swallowed all those of both nations whom war had carried off; their glory had departed.

17

Deprived of friends, the warriors left for their homes in Frisia. Yet, during that slaughter-stained winter, Hengest stayed with Finn in the homes and high city, in great misery, though he could have driven his ring-prowed ship over the sea. The ocean surged with storms, contending with the wind; winter locked the waves in its icy bond, until the new year came to the dwellings of men—as it still does now; the glorious bright weather holds to its proper time. Then winter was shaken off, the bosom of earth fair, and the exile was eager to leave the dwelling of his host.

But he wanted vengeance even more than the sea voyage. He wanted to bring about a war-council where he might bring to mind the sons of the giants. Therefore he did not refuse to do as the world advises when Hunlafing put the Battleflame, best of swords, on his lap; that blade was well known among the giants.

Thus in his turn bold Finn also met with death by the sword in his own home, when Guthlaf and Oslaf had complained of the grim attack after the sea voyage, blamed it for many woes, and the restless spirit in the heart could forbear no longer. Then the hall was reddened with the life's blood of enemies; Finn, the king, was slain with his band and the queen taken. The Danish warriors took all the king's household property to the ships—all the precious jewels they could find in Finn's home. They brought the noble wife over the sea to the Danes, and led her to her people.

The lay was sung; the gleeman's tale was over. Mirth was renewed and the noise of men at the bench resounded as cupbearers poured wine from wonderful vessels. Then Wealhtheow, wearing a golden circlet, came forward to where the two leaders, Hrothgar and his nephew, sat; at that time there was still peace between them, each one was true to the other. Unferth, the orator, sat at the feet of the Danish lord; each of them trusted his spirit, and believed that he had great courage, although he may not have been honorable in swordplay with his kinsmen. The lady of the Danes then spoke: "Take this cup, my dear sovereign lord, giver of treasure. Rejoice, generous friend of men, and speak to the Geats with words of friendship, as you should. Be gracious to the Geats, remembering how many gifts you have gathered from far and near.

"Someone has told me that you wish to have this hero as a son. Heorot is cleansed, the bright ring-hall; make use of generous rewards while you can, but leave the people and kingdom to your kinfolk when the fated time comes for you to depart. I know my gracious Hrothulf; he will protect our children honorably, if you, friend of the Scyldings, should leave this world before he does. I expect that he will well repay our children if he recalls all the kindnesses we did for him as a child, to his pleasure and honor."

Then she turned to the bench where her sons,

Hrethric and Hrothmund, were seated with other young warriors, sons of heroes; there Beowulf, the brave Geat, sat by the two brothers.

18

The cup was carried to him and cordially offered along with wrought gold, presented graciously: two arm ornaments, mail, rings, and the greatest collar I have ever heard of on earth; I have heard of no better treasure under the sky in any hoard of heroes since Hama[15] carried away the necklace of the Brisings to the glorious stronghold—he took the precious gems in their fine settings and fled Ermanaric's crafty enmity; he chose gain. Hygelac, king of the Geats, Swerting's kinsman, had that circlet with him on his last campaign, when he defended the treasure under his banner and guarded the spoil of battle. Destiny took him off when in his pride he courted trouble and made war on the Frisians. When he bore the treasure with its precious stones over the waves, the powerful lord fell there beneath his shield. The king's body with his coat of mail and the circlet as well passed into the power of the Franks. Lesser warriors plundered the slain after the slaughter of the battle, when the corpses of the Geatish people covered the battlefield.

The hall rang with applause. Wealhtheow said before the company, "Enjoy this circlet, beloved Beowulf, in all prosperity; make use of this precious mail, and prosper well; show your strength, and be a kind counselor to these boys. I will remember to reward you for it. You have brought it about that men will always honor you, near and far—even as far as the sea, home

---

[15]A legendary Germanic hero; the treasure he is said to have stolen from Ermanaric (the historical king of the East Goths) is probably a magic necklace made, according to some sources, for the goddess Freyja by the Brisings.

of the winds, encircles the shore. Be blessed as long as
you live, prince! It is proper that I grant you precious
treasure. Be gracious in deeds to my son, fortunate
one! Here each nobleman is true to the other, kindly in
spirit and loyal to his liege lord; the thanes are united,
the people of good will; the retainers have their fill of
wine and do as I bid."

Then she went to her seat. The choicest of ban-
quets was before them, and the men enjoyed the wine.
They did not know the doom, grim destiny, which
many of the nobles would meet when evening came,
and great Hrothgar went to his dwelling to take his
rest.

A countless number of noblemen inhabited the
building, as they had often done before. They cleared
away the bench planks and spread out beds and cush-
ions. One of the beer drinkers turned to his rest in the
hall doomed, ready to die. They placed their shining
wooden shields at their heads, and on the bench over
each warrior could be seen his towering war helmet
and his mail and mighty spear; it was their custom to
be always ready for war, whether at home or away,
whenever their liege lord should have need of them—it
was a good band.

Grendel's Mother Attacks

19

They sank down to fall asleep. One paid dearly for
that evening's rest, as had often been the case before
when Grendel occupied the gold hall and committed
evil, until the end came and he met death after all his
crimes. Now it became clear and obvious to everyone
that an avenger had survived the hateful monster, and
still lived after the terrible struggle was over. Grendel's
mother, a she-monster, brooded over her misery.

She was among those who had had to live in the
dreadful cold water, ever since Cain murdered his own
brother, his father's son, and went forth outlawed,
branded a murderer, to flee the joys of men and in-
habit the wastelands. He was the ancestor of many
doomed spirits, of whom Grendel, the hateful, accursed
oppressor, was one: he who found a wakeful man await-
ing battle at Heorot. There the monster had laid hold
of him, but he remembered his mighty strength, that
liberal gift which God had given him, and trusted him-
self to the Almighty for grace, help, and support. Thus
Beowulf had overcome the fiend and subdued the hell-
ish spirit. Humiliated and cut off from joy, the enemy
of mankind then departed to seek his deathbed. Still,
his mother, gloomy and greedy, intended to go on a
sorry journey to avenge her son's death.

And so she came to Heorot, where the Danes slept
about the hall: those noblemen there suffered a sudden
reverse of fortune when Grendel's mother came in.
Their terror was less by just as much as a woman's
strength in war is less in comparison with that of armed
men, when the trusty edge of the hammer-forged sword,
stained with blood, cuts against the boar over the hel-
met. Then blades were drawn in the hall, swords brought
down from over the seats, and many a shield was raised
firmly in hand—but no one thought of helmet or coat
of mail when the sudden horror seized him.

She had to hurry: she wanted to get out of there
and save her life when she had been discovered. Quick-
ly, she seized one of the warriors in a firm grasp, then
went to the fen. The man she killed in his resting-place
was a glorious hero and dearest to Hrothgar of all the
counselors in the world. Beowulf was not there: after
the treasure giving, another lodging had been assigned
to the glorious Geat.

There was an outcry in Heorot. She took the famil-
iar hand covered with blood. New sorrow had come

again to the building; nor did anyone benefit from the exchange, for on both sides they had to pay with the lives of friends.

The wise old king, the gray-haired warrior, was sad at heart when he knew that his chief thane lay lifeless, that his dearest retainer was dead. Beowulf, the man blessed with victory, was quickly summoned to his chamber. At daybreak the noble champion went with his companions to where the venerable king was waiting and wondering whether the Almighty would ever work a change for him, as he pondered the sad tidings. The hero went across the floor with his troop—the wood of the hall resounded—and, in response to the summons, greeted the Danish ruler, asking him whether the night had been pleasant.

20

Hrothgar, protector of the Scyldings, spoke: "Do not ask about pleasure! The sorrow of the Danish people is renewed. Aeschere is dead—Yrmenlaf's older brother, my confidant and counselor and my comrade in arms when we defended our heads in battle where troops clashed and struck against the boar-helmets. A nobleman should be such as Aeschere was—an excellent prince! A restless murderous demon has killed him in Heorot.

"I do not know where the horrible being went, glorying in carrion and glad of prey. She avenged the death of Grendel, whom you killed violently with your handgrasp last night, because he had too long diminished and destroyed my people. He fell in war, his life forfeit. And now another has come, a mighty, wicked ravager who wishes to avenge her kinsman—and has gone far indeed to even the feud, as it may seem to many a thane who mourns in his heart for the generous patron. It is a sore distress of spirit, for now that hand which was wont to give you everything you wished lies low.

"I have heard my people, countrymen, and counselors say that they saw two such great wanderers, alien spirits, keeping the moor. One of them, as they could definitely see, was in the likeness of a woman; the other wretched creature trod the paths of exile in the form of a man, except that he was larger than any other man. Him, the countrymen used to call Grendel. They know nothing of his father, nor whether other evil spirits preceded him. They inhabit uncharted country, the retreat of wolves: windy cliffs and dangerous fen paths, where a mountain stream goes down under the misty bluffs and the flood runs under the earth. It is not many miles from here that the mere stands. Over it hang frosty groves, the firmly rooted wood shadowing the water. Every night a fearful wonder can be seen there: fire on the water.

"There is no man alive who knows the bottom of that mere. Although the antlered hart, when pursued by hounds and driven far over the heath, may seek out the forest, still he will sooner give up his life on the bank than jump in to save his head. That is not a safe place. There surging water rises up dark towards the clouds when wind stirs up hateful storms, until the air becomes gloomy and the heavens weep. Now, again, you alone can help. You do not know that region, the dangerous place where you might find the polluted creature: seek it if you dare! I will reward you for the fight with riches of twisted gold and ancient treasure, as I did before, if you get away."

21

Beowulf, son of Ecgtheow, spoke in reply: "Do not sorrow, wise lord! It is better for a man to avenge his friend rather than to mourn greatly. Each of us must expect an end of this world's life. Let him who can acquire glory before death; that is best for a warrior in the end, when life is gone. Rise, protector of the kingdom: let us go quickly and look at the track of Grendel's kinswoman. I promise this to you: she shall not escape to cover, neither in the bosom of the earth nor in the mountain wood, nor on the bottom of the ocean—go where she will. Have patience this day with all your sorrows as I expect you to."

The old man then sprang up and thanked God, the mighty Lord, for the hero's words.

A horse with twisted mane was bridled for Hrothgar and the wise prince went forth in a stately manner. A band on foot advanced, bearing shields. They saw many tracks along the paths of the wood, along the ground where she had journeyed directly forward over the murky moor bearing the lifeless body of the best thane of all those that ruled at home with Hrothgar. The king went over steep stone cliffs and along narrow paths where it was necessary to go one by one, along unknown ways, over steep bluffs and past many dens of water monsters; with a few experienced men he went on in front to examine the place, until he suddenly found mountain trees leaning over gray stones, a joyless wood. The water stood below, bloody and turbid. It was a painful thing for all the Danes to suffer, a great grief to every thane, when they encountered Aeschere's head on the waterside cliff.

The water boiled with blood, hot gore, as the people gazed at it. From time to time a horn sounded an eager battle song. The troop all sat down, and saw in the water many serpents, strange sea dragons exploring the brine, and water monsters lying on the slopes of the bluff, the kind that many a morning take their ill-omened way on the high sea—such serpents and wild beasts. They rushed away in bitter fury when they heard the clear song of the war horn.

One of the Geatish men took his bow and ended
the life of one of the creatures swimming in the waves,
for a hard battle-arrow penetrated to its life and it was
the slower in making its way through the water as
death took it off—it was soon hard pressed in the waves
with boar spears, savagely barbed; the wondrous wave-
roamer, fiercely attacked, was drawn to the cliff. The
men gazed at the frightful enemy.

Beowulf arrayed himself in noble armor—he did
not worry about his life at all. His broad and well-
woven coat of mail was to try out the waters—that
garment which could protect his body so that the grip
of battle could not injure his breast, the malicious grasp
of the angry foe could not harm his life. His head was
protected by his shining helmet, which was to stir up
the bottom of the mere, to seek the surging water; it
was enriched with treasure and encircled with a splen-
did band, as the smith had made it in far-off days,
when he fashioned it wonderfully and adorned it with
swine images so that afterwards no sword could bite
through it.

And, in his need, Unferth, Hrothgar's orator, loaned
him a weapon that was not the least of helps: Hrunting
was the name of the hilted sword. That was among the
best of ancient treasures. The edge was iron, colored
with poison-stripes, hardened with blood shed in battle—
never had it failed any of the men who grasped it in
their hands, this sword which dared to go on the peril-
ous expedition to the hostile dwelling; it was not the
first time that it was to perform valorous deeds. In-
deed, as Ecglaf's mighty kinsman lent the weapon to
the better swordsman, he gave no thought to what he
had said before when he was drunk with wine; he
himself did not dare to venture his life to accomplish
deeds of valor under the waves. Thus he lost an oppor-
tunity to win glory and fame for courage. It was not so
with the other, when he had arrayed himself for fighting.

The Battle at the Bottom of the Mere

22

Beowulf, son of Ecgtheow, spoke: "Wise and generous prince, glorious son of Healfdene, remember, now that I am ready for the venture, what we two said earlier: that if I should lose my life for your sake, you would always stand in a father's place to me when I am gone. Be a protector to my retainers and companions if battle should take me. Also, beloved Hrothgar, send the treasures you gave to me on to Hygelac; then the lord of the Geats, the son of Hrethel, can see, when he looks at the golden treasure, that I found a lord of great munificence and enjoyed it while I could. And let Unferth have my ancient sword, the splendid heirloom with wavy ornament; that renowned man may have the hard blade. Either I will gain fame with Hrunting or death shall carry me off."

After these words, the leader of the Geats pressed on courageously—he did not want to wait for an answer. The surging water received the warrior. It was a good part of the day before he could see the bottom. Soon the grim and greedy monster, who had occupied the watery regions for a hundred half-years, found that a man was exploring the alien region from above. She grasped at him, and grabbed the hero in her horrible claws—but nevertheless she could not harm his body, which was unhurt because mail protected it all about; her hostile fingers could not penetrate the war shirt, the intertwined coat of mail.

When she reached the bottom, the she-wolf of the water bore the armed chieftain to her dwelling in such a way that, courageous as he was, he could not use his weapons. Many strange beings afflicted him in the water; many a sea beast tried to break his battle coat with its

warlike tusks; many monsters pursued him. Then the
hero saw that he was in some sort of enemy hall, where
no water harmed him at all and its sudden rush could
not touch him because of the roof of the chamber; he
saw firelight, brilliant flames shining brightly.

Now the brave man could see the accursed mon-
ster of the deep, the mighty mere-woman. He did not
hold back his blow, but gave a mighty rush with his
sword so that the blade sang a fierce war song on her
head. But the stranger found that the flashing sword
would not bite or do her harm; the edge failed the
prince in his need. It had endured many skirmishes
before and had often sheared the helmet and mail of a
doomed man: this was the first time that the glory of
the precious treasure was diminished.

But the kinsman of Hygelac was resolute and in-
tent on achieving brave deeds; his courage did not fail
him at all. The angry warrior threw the ornamented
sword so that the firm steel edge lay on the earth; he
trusted in his own strength, his mighty handgrip. So
must a man do when he hopes to gain long-lasting
fame in war—he cannot worry about saving his life.
The leader of the Geats did not flinch from the battle:
he seized Grendel's mother by the shoulder. In a fury,
the bold warrior flung the deadly foe so that she fell to
the floor. She quickly retaliated with grim grasps and
seized him; weary in spirit, the strongest of champions
stumbled and fell down.

The demon pounced on the intruder, drew her
knife, broad and bright of edge—she wished to avenge
her child, her only son. The woven mail which covered
Beowulf's shoulder protected his life and withstood
the entry of point and edge. Ecgtheow's son, the
Geatish champion, would have perished then under
the earth if his armor, the hard war mail, had not
given him help; and holy God brought about vic-

tory in battle. The wise Lord, Ruler of the heavens, easily decided the issue rightly, after Beowulf stood up again.

23

Among the armor in that place he saw a victorious sword: an ancient giant's sword, strong of edge, the glory of warriors. It was the choicest of weapons except that this good and splendid work of giants was too huge for any other man to carry in battle. The grim, fierce defender of the Danes seized the chained hilt and drew the ring-marked sword, despairing of life; angrily he struck so that it took her hard against the neck and broke the bone-rings. The sword cut right through her doomed body and she fell to the floor. The sword was bloody; the man rejoiced in his work.

A light gleamed; a glow shone forth within, just as the sun, candle of the skies, shines brightly from heaven. Beowulf looked around the building and turned along the wall. Hygelac's thane raised the weapon firmly by the hilt, angry and determined—that blade was not useless to the warrior, for he wished to repay Grendel at once for the many attacks which he had made on the Danes, many besides that first time when he killed Hrothgar's men in their sleep, ate fifteen sleeping men of the Danish tribe and carried off as many again, hideous booty! The fierce warrior had repaid him for that so that now he found Grendel lying in his resting-place, wearied by war, dead of his injuries at the fight in Heorot. The corpse burst wide open when it suffered a blow after death; Beowulf cut off its head with a hard stroke of the sword.

Now the observant men who watched the mere with Hrothgar saw that the surging water was turbulent and stained with blood. The gray-haired veterans consulted together about the brave warrior, saying that they did not expect to see the noble man again; they did not think he would return in victory to their glorious prince. Many were agreed that the sea wolf must have destroyed him. Then came the ninth hour of the day.

The valiant Danes left the slope; the generous lord departed to return home. The foreigners sat sick at heart and stared at the mere; they wished to see their dear lord himself, but they did not expect it.

Meanwhile, because of the blood shed, the sword began to shrink; the weapon looked like an icicle of battle. That was a great marvel: it melted just as ice does, when the Father releases the bond of frost; he who has power over times and seasons unbinds the fetters of the water—that is the true Creator. The chief of the Geats did not take any more of the valuable property in the cavern, although he saw many things there; he took only the head and ornamented hilt. The sword had already melted. The decorated blade had burnt up in the hot blood of the poisonous alien spirit who had died there. Soon the victor who had seen his foes fall in battle was swimming again. He dove up through the water; the great expanse of the mere was completely cleansed when the monster had ended the days of its life and left this transitory world.

The seafarer came swimming to land. The stout-hearted man rejoiced in the booty he brought from the sea, that great burden which he had with him. The group of mighty thanes went towards him and thanked God, rejoicing to see their lord safe and sound. The champion's helmet and coat of mail were quickly loosened from him. The lake grew torpid; the water, stained with the blood of battle, lay still under the clouds.

The valiant band set forth along the footpath, and went back rejoicing on the well-known roads. The bold men bore the head from the waterside cliff, but with

great difficulty—it took the labors of four men to bear
Grendel's head to the hall on the shaft of a spear.

Presently the fourteen brave, warlike Geats came
to the hall; the courageous leader crossed the cleared
area around the mead-hall with the rest of his troop
and entered in. That daring man, honored for his
glorious deeds, went to greet Hrothgar. Grendel's head
was carried by the hair out upon the hall floor there
where men drank, before the lords and their queen:
the men gazed at the wondrous sight.

Heorot Cleansed

24

Beowulf, son of Ecgtheow, spoke: "Behold, son of
Healfdene, lord of the Danes, we have gladly brought
you these sea spoils which you see here as a sign of
success. I barely escaped with my life from the fight
under the water: the battle would have been lost at
once if God had not shielded me. I could not do any-
thing in battle with Hrunting, although it is a good
weapon. But the Ruler of men, who has often guided
those who are friendless, granted that I might see a
beautiful sword, a huge heirloom, hanging on the wall;
so I drew that weapon. Then, when I had an opportu-
nity, I killed the guardian of the house. But the blade,
with its interlaced markings, burned up as the blood,
the hottest of battle gore, sprang out.

"I carried off the hilt from the enemies; I had
avenged their wicked deeds, the slaughter of Danes, as
was fitting. Now I promise you that you can sleep in
Heorot free from care among your band of men, with
all your thanes, the veterans and the youth; and that
you, lord of the Danes, need not dread injury to them,
death to your court, from that quarter, as you did
before."

Then he gave the golden hilt, made by giants long ago, into the hand of the gray-haired chief; the work of wonderful smiths came into the possession of the lord of the Danes after the downfall of the demons. That malicious creature, God's adversary, left this world, guilty of murder, and his mother with him; then the sword hilt came into the keeping of that best of earthly kings between two seas, of those who gave out treasure in the Danish realm.

Hrothgar spoke. He gazed at the hilt, the old heirloom on which was written the story of the beginning of ancient strife when the flood struck and the sea poured over the race of giants—they suffered terribly. That was a race estranged from the eternal Lord, but in the end the Ruler punished them through the flood of the water. On the bright-gold sword guard it was also set down and marked correctly in runic letters for whom that sword was first made, that choicest of iron weapons with its twisted hilt and serpentine ornamentation.

Then the wise king spoke, and all were silent: "Indeed, one who works right and truth among the people, an old guardian of the land who has a long memory, can say that this lord was born a better man. My friend Beowulf, your glory is established far and wide, over all nations. You carry all your might steadily, with discretion of mind. I shall carry out the agreement we made before. You shall be a long-lasting comfort to your people, a help to warriors.

"Heremod was not so to the children of Ecgwela, the glorious Scyldings; he turned out to accomplish not their joy, but the slaughter and death of the Danish people. He killed his boon companions in his rages—his own close friends, until the ill-famed prince was exiled from human joys. Although mighty God raised him beyond all men in the enjoyment of power and might, nevertheless a bloodthirsty heart grew within his breast. He gave no rings to the Danes in order to win glory. He lived joyless, and suffered the result of strife, long, great affliction. Learn by this: understand manly virtue. I, being old in winters, tell this tale for your sake.

"It is wonderful to tell how mighty God, through his great magnanimous spirit, distributes wisdom, land, and noble rank among mankind; he has power over all. Sometimes he lets the spirit of a man of high descent meet every pleasure: gives him earthly joy in his homeland and a stronghold of men to hold: and renders regions of the world, a broad realm, so subject to him that in his folly he cannot imagine an end. His life is a perpetual feast; sickness and old age do not hinder him a bit, no trouble casts a shadow in his heart, nor does strife bring about fighting anywhere—the whole world bends to do his will. He knows nothing of a worse condition.

25

"But arrogance grows and flourishes within him; then the guardian, the keeper of the soul, sleeps. That sleep is too sound, and hedged about with troubles; the killer who shoots wickedly from his bow is very near. Then he cannot protect himself; he is struck in the breast with bitter arrows which no armor stops, the perverse and strange commands of the accursed spirit. That which he has held too long seems to him too little; he is niggardly and surly; he does not give out gold-plated rings honorably, and he forgets his latter end and does not think of the honors which God, the Lord of glory, gave him earlier. In the end it comes about that his mortal body withers and falls doomed; another succeeds him, one who gives out treasure without grieving—he does not guard the noble heirlooms anxiously!

   "Keep yourself from such wickedness, dear Beowulf, best of men; choose what is better: eternal gains! Shun arrogance, famous champion. Now you are at the height of your power for a while, but before long it shall come to pass that illness or the sword will cut off your strength—or the fire will grip you, or flooding waters, or the attack with a knife, or the flight of spears, or dire old age; or perhaps the brightness of your eyes will lessen and become dim; presently death will overpower you, brave warrior.

   "For a hundred seasons now I have governed the Danes under the heavens and protected them in war from many nations around this earth, from ashen spears and sword blades, so that I did not count any under the compass of the skies as my adversary. But I suffered a reversal in my own home: sorrow succeeded joy when Grendel, enemy of men, invaded my hall; I suffered continual distress because of his persecution.

   "Now may God, the eternal Lord, be thanked for this: that I have lived to gaze with my own eyes on that bloodstained head after the former strife! Now go to your seat and enjoy the pleasures of the banquet, victorious hero. We two shall share a great many treasures when morning comes."

   The Geat was glad at heart and quickly went to seek out his seat, as the wise king bade him. Then again, as before, a feast was handsomely set forth in the hall for the valiant warriors.

   The cover of night grew deeper, dark over the troop of men. All the retainers arose, for the grayhaired old man of the Scyldings wished to go to his bed. The brave Geat warrior had great need of rest and, weary after his adventure, he was quickly led out by the chamberlains who attended courteously to all the needs which a seafaring nobleman would have had in those days.

   Then the great-hearted man rested in the towering

building, vaulted and decorated with gold; there the
guest slept until the black raven blithely announced
heaven's joy. Then the light came quickly, brightness
drove away the shadows. The warriors made haste, for
the princes were eager to travel home to their people,
and the hero wished to return to his distant ship.

Then the brave man ordered Hrunting brought to
Ecglaf's son, and told him to receive his sword, the
precious iron weapon. He gave him thanks for the loan
of it, saying that he valued it as a good friend in battle,
powerful in war; he did not find fault with the sword's
edge. He was a man of noble spirit.

The warriors were ready in their armor, eager to
depart. Now the prince dear to the Danes went to the
high seat where the king sat. The hero brave in battle
greeted Hrothgar.

26

Beowulf, son of Ecgtheow, spoke: "We seafarers
from far away wish to say that we are eager to return to
Hygelac. We were well entertained here in every re-
spect; you have treated us well. If I can do anything on
earth, lord of men, to earn more of your love with
warlike deeds than I have yet done, I am ready at once.
If I hear over the seas that neighbors threaten you with
terror, as enemies did before, I will bring you a thou-
sand thanes, heroes, to help you. Although Hygelac,
lord of the Geats, is young, I know that the people's
guardian will help me with words and deeds, so that I
may honor you well and bear a spear to help you when
you have need of men. If, then, Hrethric, your son,
should decide to go to the court of the Geats, he will
find many friends there; other countries are best vis-
ited by a man who is himself accomplished."

Hrothgar answered him, "The wise Lord sent these
words into your mind. Never have I heard so young a

man speak so wisely! You are strong in might and sage
in mind, wise speaker. I expect that if it happens that
the spear of grim warfare, disease or steel, should take
Hrethel's son, your lord, the people's guardian, while
you are alive, the Geats have none better to choose as
king and guardian of their treasure if you will rule the
realm of your kin.

"Your spirit pleases me more the longer I know
you, dear Beowulf. You have brought it about that there
shall be peace between our peoples, the Geats and the
Danes; there shall be no more of the strife and hostile
acts which they endured before. As long as I govern
this realm we shall exchange treasures; many men shall
greet each other over the water with good things, the
ring-prowed ship shall bring gifts and signs of friend-
ship over the sea. I know the people are steadfast in
both enmity and friendship, blameless in every way,
according to ancient custom."

Then the protector of noblemen gave Beowulf
twelve more treasures, and bade him go safely to his
people with the treasure and quickly return again. Then
the most noble lord of the Scyldings kissed that best of
thanes and clasped him by the neck; tears fell from the
eyes of the gray-haired king. The wise old man knew
there were two possibilities, but he thought one most
likely: that they would not see each other again. The
man was so dear to him that he could not hold back his
emotion, for in his breast, firm in his heart, affection
for the hero moved him.

Splendidly decked with gold, Beowulf left him, and
went over the grassy earth, exulting in his treasure.
The ship, riding at anchor, awaited its owner. As they
went, Hrothgar's gift was praised; he was a king blame-
less in every way, until old age, which often harms
many, robbed him of his might.

Beowulf's Homecoming

27

The courageous troop of young men came to the water, wearing their coats of ring-mail. The coast guard saw the band returning, as before he had seen them arrive. He did not greet the visitors with threats from the brow of the cliff, but rode towards them, saying that these warriors going to the ship in their bright armor would be indeed welcomed by the Geatish people. The broad vessel on the beach was laden with battle gear; the ring-prowed ship was filled with horses and treasures—the mast towered over Hrothgar's hoard of precious things. Beowulf gave the guard a sword wound with gold, so that afterwards he was the more honored on the mead-bench because of that heirloom treasure.

The ship went out, stirring up the deep water, and left the Danish land. A cloth sail was raised on the mast and made fast with rope. The wooden ship groaned. No wind over the waves drove her from her course and the vessel proceeded, floated foamy-necked over the waves; the ship with its bound prow went forward over the ocean streams until they could see the Geatish cliffs, the familiar headlands.

Driven by the wind, the keel pressed on until it stood on the land. Quickly the harbor guard came to the shore—for a long time now he had eagerly looked out far from the beach for these beloved men. He moored the great ship to the beach and made it fast with anchor ropes, so that the force of the waves could not drive the vessel away from them.

Beowulf ordered the noble treasure, precious things and plated gold, carried up. He had not far to go to find his lord, Hygelac, son of Hrethel, for he and his

comrades dwelt near the sea wall. Hygelac's hall was
splendid, the king valiant and noble, and the queen
very young: Hygd was wise and accomplished, although
Haereth's daughter had not lived many winters within
the hall-fort. She was not mean and niggardly with gifts
of valuable treasure to the Geatish people.

She was not like the proud queen Modthryth, who
committed terrible crimes. No brave courtier dared be
so bold as to stare openly at her when he was not her
lord; if he did, he knew that bonds of death were in
store for him—soon after he was seized, a knife would
be brought; the ornamented sword would settle the
matter. Death would be the upshot. Such a custom is
not fitting for a queen, even though she is beautiful; it
is not queenly for a gentle lady to deprive a good man
of his life because of pretended insult.

However, Hemming's kinsman, Offa,[16] stopped all
that. Men told another tale over the ale-bench: that she
brought about fewer killings and evil acts after she was
given, decked with gold, to that most noble young
champion, when, according to her father's bidding, she
made a journey over the yellow-green sea to Offa's hall.
There she made good use of her destined life on the
throne, and as long as she lived she was famed for her
goodness, and held great love for that chief of heroes,
who was, they say, the best of all men between two seas.
Offa was widely exalted for his generosity and success
in war; the bold man governed his native land wisely.
To them was born Eomor, help of heroes, kinsman of
Hemming, and grandson of Garmund; a warrior skill-
ful in battle.

---

[16]A legendary prehistoric king of the continental Angles, considered to be
the ancestor of the historical Offa, king of Mercia (d. 796).

Beowulf and his companions went off along the
sand; they trod along the sea strand, the wide shores,
as the sun, light of the world, came hastening from the
south. They went on quickly to the place where they
understood that their good young warrior-king, slayer
of Ongentheow, dealt out rings within his stronghold.
Hygelac was told at once of Beowulf's arrival; he learned
that the hero, his comrade in arms, came into the
enclosure alive, returning safely to the court from the
battle. Quickly room in the hall was yielded to the
troop, according to the king's orders.

Beowulf, back from his perilous journey, sat down
with his kinsman, Hygelac, after his ruler had greeted
him ceremoniously with earnest words. Haereth's daugh-
ter passed around the hall with mead cups; she treated
the people kindly and put the cup of strong drink in
the warrior's hands.

Hygelac, who burned with curiosity, began to ques-
tion his comrade about the seafaring Geat's adven-
tures: "What happened to you on your journey, dear
Beowulf, when you suddenly determined to seek out
strife far away over the salt water and join battle at
Heorot? Have you in any way remedied princely
Hrothgar's well-known trouble? I brooded over your
venture in great distress and sorrow; I had no faith in
my dear friend's undertaking, and for a long time I
entreated you not to approach the murderous demon
at all, but to let the Danes settle the fight with Grendel
themselves. I give thanks to God that I may see you
safe and sound."

Beowulf, Ecgtheow's son, spoke: "My encounter
with Grendel is no secret, lord Hygelac; many men
have heard what a fight between us two took place
there where he had brought such sorrow and misery to

so many of the victorious Scyldings. I avenged all that, so that none of Grendel's kin on earth—whichever of that hateful race, enveloped in crime, lives longest—need boast of that night's clash.

"First, I went to the hall to greet Hrothgar. When the glorious son of Healfdene knew my intentions, he assigned me a seat beside his own son at once. The company was merry; never in the world have I seen a court enjoy themselves more over the mead. From time to time the splendid queen, the people's peacemaker, passed all around the hall urging the young men to drink, and gave twisted rings to many a man before she took her seat.

"At times, Hrothgar's daughter came before the veterans and bore the ale cup to all the noblemen in succession—I heard the hall dwellers call her Freawaru as she gave the studded vessel to the heroes. Young and gold adorned, she is betrothed to Ingeld,[17] the gracious son of Froda. The protector of the Scyldings, the nation's guardian, has agreed to this; he considers it a good plan to settle many quarrels and deadly feuds by means of the woman. But it is very seldom that the deadly spear rests for long after a king has fallen, however admirable the bride may be.

"For it may displease the prince of the Heathobards (and all that nation's thanes) when the Danish attendant goes into the hall with his lady and they are splendidly entertained.

---

[17]King of the Heathobards, enemies of the Danes, who had killed his father, Froda. Beowulf's prophecy of the failure of Hrothgar's attempt to settle the feud by marrying his daughter to Ingeld is no doubt true: from other sources we gather that it was a raid of the Heathobards which caused the burning of Heorot.

[29]

"On the Danes shine heirlooms which once belonged to the Heathobards: the strong, ring-decorated treasure that their ancestors owned while they could wield weapons, until they led their comrades to destruction in the shieldplay and forfeited their very lives. —Then, over the beer, looking at the treasure, an old warrior speaks, one who remembers everything about how men fell by the spear; a man grim of spirit.

"In his bitterness, he begins to try the temper of a young warrior with his secret thoughts in order to arouse war, and he says these words: 'My friend, do you recognize the sword which your father bore to battle when he wore his grim helmet for the last time— the excellent blade he had there where the Danes slew him? The bold Scyldings held the battlefield when Withergyld lay dead, and our heroes had fallen. Now the son of one of the killers goes about here on our hall floor exulting in that prize; he boasts of the murder and bears the treasure which you, by right, should possess.'

"Thus, he urges him and continually reminds him with bitter words, until the time shall come when the woman's thane lies covered with blood, slaughtered with a stroke of the sword, his life forfeited because of his father's deeds; while the other escapes from there alive, for he knows that land well. Then on both sides the oaths of lords are broken and Ingeld seethes with deadly hate; his love for his wife shall be cooled by the waves of sorrow.

"Because this is likely to happen, I do not consider the friendship of the Heathobards firm or their alliance with the Danes secure.

"Now I shall go on and tell you about Grendel, so that you, lord, may know what came of the mighty combat. After the sun set, the angry demon came; the terrible night prowler sought us out where we, as yet unharmed, guarded the hall. His attack there was fatal to Hondscio—a deadly encounter for the doomed man. That champion was the first victim, and Grendel devoured the famous thane—he swallowed all of the good man's body. Yet the bloody-toothed slayer, his mind set on destruction, was none the readier to leave the hall empty-handed.

"Confident of his own strength, he decided to try me, and grasped at me eagerly. His glove hung down, wide and strange, fastened with wonderfully made clasps—it was all cunningly made by the skill of a devil, from dragon skins. The fierce evildoer wanted to put me in there as one of many innocent victims. This could not be when I stood up in anger.

[30]

"It would take too long to tell how I repaid the enemy of men for each of his evil acts; but, my prince, my deeds there exalted the reputation of your people. He escaped and enjoyed the privilege of life for a little while; but his right hand stayed behind at Heorot, and he was driven away abject, to fall in misery to the bottom of a mere.

"The lord of the Danes rewarded me with gold and many treasures, when the next day came and we sat down to the banquet. There was singing and merriment. The venerable king of the Scyldings told of days gone by; at times the brave warrior played the harp delightfully, or told a tale, both true and sad; at times the great-hearted king, stiffened by age, would begin to mourn his youth and strength in battle: his heart was stirred as the aged man remembered many things.

"And so we took our pleasure there all day long,

until another night came to men. Then Grendel's mother was quickly ready for revenge; she came mourning, for death—and the bitter hatred of the Geats—had taken away her son. The she-monster avenged her child and boldly killed a man. There Aeschere, a sage counselor, was deprived of life. But when morning came the Danish people could not burn the death-wearied man in the fire nor put their dear friend on the funeral pyre; for she bore off the body under the mountain stream in her fiendish grasp. For Hrothgar, that was the bitterest of the many sorrows which had long afflicted the ruler.

"Then the unhappy lord implored me by your life to undertake a heroic task in the tumultuous water, to risk my life and do glorious deeds; he promised me reward. Then, as is widely known, I found the grim and horrible guardian of the deep in the surging water. There we were in hand-to-hand combat for some time; the water boiled with blood, and with a mighty sword I cut off the head of Grendel's mother in her hall. I barely managed to escape with my life, but I was not yet doomed; and the protector of noblemen gave me many treasures afterwards.

31

"The king thus followed courtly custom. I did not by any means lose the rewards which are the due of might; Healfdene's son gave me treasures of my own choosing. These I wish to bring to you, my king, to offer with good will. All my joys still depend on you; I have few near relatives aside from you, my Hygelac."

Beowulf ordered the men to bring in a boar-banner, a towering war helmet, a bright coat of mail, and a splendid sword; then he made this speech: "When Hrothgar gave me this battle gear, the wise prince asked me particularly to tell you its history first. He

said that King Heorogar,[18] lord of the Danes, had it for
a long time; however, he would not give the armor to
his son, bold Heoroweard, although he was a loyal son
to him. Make good use of it!"

I have heard that following these arms came four
bay horses, swift and exactly matched: Beowulf made
Hygelac a gift of both horses and treasures. This is
what kinsmen should do instead of weaving a net of
malice for each other, preparing death for their close
comrades with stealthy craft. Bold Hygelac's nephew
was most loyal to him, and each had the other's welfare
at heart.

I have heard that Beowulf gave Hygd, the prince's
daughter, the neckpiece, that splendid great treasure
which Wealhtheow had given him as well as three
graceful horses, bearing bright saddles; Hygd's breast
was well adorned after she received that gift.

Thus did Ecgtheow's son, so famous for battles
and valiant deeds, act as a brave man ought; his behav-
ior was worthy of praise. He never struck down hearth-
companions when drunk for he did not have a savage
spirit; but with the greatest of human skill the valiant
warrior took care of the liberal gifts which God had
given him. In the past he had long been despised: the
Geats did not consider him worthy, nor would the lord
of the Geats show him much favor at the mead-bench;
they thought that he was slothful, a feeble prince.—But
all the hero's troubles had come to an end.

The warlike king now ordered Hrethel's golden
legacy brought in; the Geats had no better sword than
this precious treasure. He laid it in Beowulf's lap, and
gave him seven thousand hides of land, a hall, and a
throne. Both of them held inherited land in that na-
tion, an estate, and ancestral home, but the greater
realm belonged to Hygelac since he was higher in rank.

---

[18]Elder brother of Hrothgar; see genealogical tables.

In later days it came to pass, in the clash of battle, that Hygelac lay dead and Heardred was cut down behind the shield-wall, when the warlike Swedes sought him out among his warriors and violently attacked Hereric's nephew—then the broad realm passed into Beowulf's hands. He ruled it well for fifty winters, and was then a wise king, a venerable guardian of his land, until a certain creature began a reign of terror in the dark nights: a dragon, who kept watch over a hoard of treasure in its upland lair. Below that steep stone barrow lay a path unknown to men. A certain man found his way there and groped near the heathen hoard: in his hand he took a precious treasure. The dragon then found out that he had been tricked in his sleep by the craft of the thief: the people of the neighborhood soon found out that he was enraged.

PART II: Beowulf and the Dragon

The Dragon's Hoard

32

The thief did not break into the dragon's hoard of his own accord; he who injured the dragon so sorely did it not of his own free will, but in sore distress. A slave of a certain man, he had fled from hateful blows and was in need of a refuge. The guilty man penetrated into the dragon's lair where he soon found that a terrible horror lay in wait for the stranger. Nevertheless, in his fear the wretched man took the treasure.

There were many such ancient treasures in that earth mound, for in days of old a certain careful man had hidden the precious riches there, the immense legacy of a noble race. Death had carried off the rest in earlier times, and the veteran of that band who lived the longest, guarding the wealth and mourning his friends, expected that the same fate would come to him, and that he would have very little time to enjoy the long-accumulated wealth.

Nearby, on the plain near the waves of the water, was a barrow, newly built by the headlands and made difficult of access. There the guardian of the rings took a great quantity of noble golden treasure, well worthy of being hoarded, and said these words: "Earth, guard the wealth of princes, now that warriors cannot. Indeed, it was from you that men won it earlier; now death in battle, fearful slaughter, has taken them off, and all of my people have left this life—they have seen the last of the joys of the hall.

"I have no one who can bear a sword or polish a precious drinking cup; the host has gone to another place. The strong helmet adorned with gold must be deprived of its adornment, for those whose duty it was to polish the armor now sleep; likewise the mail, which once endured the bite of iron weapons over clashing shields in battle, now crumbles away as the men did; never again can it travel afar with the warriors, side by side with heroes. The harp is no longer joyous; there is no merry song; no good hawk swings through the hall, nor does the swift horse beat his feet in the courtyard. Baleful death has banished many of the race of men."

Thus the last survivor of them all mournfully bewailed his sorrows; cheerless, he kept on, day and night, until the tide of death touched his heart.

The old oppressor of the night found the hoard standing open: he who, burning, seeks out barrows, the bare, malicious dragon who flies by night, surrounded by fire; the country dwellers dread him greatly. He looks for the hoard in the earth, where, old in winters, he guards the heathen gold—but he is not a bit better off for it.

For three hundred winters the despoiler of the people guarded that great treasure house in the earth, until a certain man infuriated him when he took the dragon's golden cup to his master, asking his lord for a compact of peace. He explored the hoard and carried off the treasure; and when his lord looked at the ancient work of men for the first time, the wretched man's boon was granted. Then the serpent awoke, and the trouble began.

The bold beast quickly moved among the stones and found the footprints of his enemy, who had stepped forward, with stealthy craft, near the dragon's head— one who is not doomed can easily pass through woe and misery unharmed, if he has the Ruler's favor. The guardian of the hoard searched eagerly along the ground: he wanted to find the man who had robbed him in his sleep. Burning, angry, he cast about the cave again and again in all directions—while he could find no man in that wilderness, he was more and more in the mood for battle. Many times he turned back to the barrow and looked for the precious cup, but he soon found that someone had tampered with the gold, his great treasure.

The guardian of the hoard waited impatiently until evening came; the vindictive barrow's watchman was enraged: he wanted to revenge the theft of the precious drinking vessel with flames. When day had gone—none too soon to suit the dragon—he had no desire to wait in his barrow, but went out surrounded by fire and armed with flames. It was a terrible beginning for the people of the land, just as the end was quick and terrible for their lord.

33

The invader began to spew forth flames, burning
the bright dwellings. The gleam of fire shone forth in
enmity to men; the hateful air-flyer would not spare
anything alive. The serpent's devastation was seen ev-
erywhere; the cruel enemy's persecution was all too
evident—all saw how the destroyer hated and humbled
the Geatish people. Then he hastened back to his hoard,
his secret hall, before daytime: he had overwhelmed
the countrymen with flame, fire, and burning, and now
he trusted in his barrow, its warlike defense and wall;
but that expectation failed him.

The extent of the horror was made clear to Beowulf
at once, for his own home, best of buildings, had been
consumed by the fire—the high throne of the Geats
was destroyed. That was a terrible grief to the good
man, the greatest of sorrows. The wise king feared that
he had bitterly angered God, the eternal Lord, by some
infringement of ancient law, and his breast seethed
within with dark thoughts, which was not customary
with him.

The fiery dragon had destroyed the people's fast-
ness with his flames, and laid waste the land near the
sea. The war king, lord of the Geats, resolved to take
revenge on him for this. He then ordered a splendid
iron shield made for him; he well knew that a wooden
shield could not help him against flame. The long-
famed nobleman was about to reach the end of his
brief, passing days, this world's life, and the serpent,
although he had guarded the hoard-wealth long, was to
go together with him. The prince scorned to seek out
the wide-flyer with a troop of men, a large army; nor
did he dread the battle for himself, or care a whit for
the serpent's strength and courage in fighting, for he
had dared great difficulty, and survived many a contest

in the crash of battle since the time when he had
victoriously cleansed Hrothgar's hall and crushed
Grendel's hateful kin in battle.

That was no minor battle, either, when Hygelac
was slain: when Hrethel's son, the people's dear lord,
was struck down by the sword and died in Friesland.
Beowulf got away from there through his own strength;
he endured a hard sea-passage. He had thirty sets of
armor on his arm when he went to the sea. Those
Hetware who came against him bearing shields had no
cause to gloat over the fight on foot: few escaped from
that warrior to seek their homes again.

Then Ecgtheow's son swam back over an expanse
of the sea to his people, a wretched solitary survivor.
There Hygd offered him the hoard and the realm,
rings and throne, for she was afraid that her child
could not hold the ancestral seat against foreign ar-
mies, now that Hygelac was dead. But nevertheless the
nobleman would not heed the pleas of the bereaved
people; not for any consideration would he be Heardred's
lord, or assume the royal power. But he supported
Heardred among the people with friendly advice, with
good will and honor, until he became older and ruled
the Geats.

Banished men, the sons of Ohthere,[19] came to
Heardred over the seas. They had rebelled against
Onela, the protector of the Swedes, that best of the sea
kings who dispensed treasure in Sweden. That caused
the end of Heardred's life; the son of Hygelac gained
nothing but a mortal wound. When Heardred lay dead,
Onela went back to his own country. Ongentheow's son
let Beowulf hold the throne and rule the Geats. That
was a good king.

---

[19] A Swedish prince (see genealogical tables); the events stemming from the
revolt of the sons of Ohthere are of major importance in Part II, since the
increasingly serious feud between the Swedes and the Geats threatens the
extinction of the Geat nation when Beowulf is dead (see Introduction).

Beowulf Goes Alone Against the Dragon

34

In later days Beowulf did not forget the duty of
revenging the death of a prince. He befriended de-
serted Eadgils, supporting the son of Ohthere beyond
the wide sea with an army, with warriors and weapons;
and Eadgils avenged the feud with devastating attacks:
he deprived King Onela of life.

Thus Ecgtheow's son had survived every battle,
each dangerous conflict, and deed of valor, until the
day came when he was to fight with the serpent. Then
the lord of the Geats, swelling with anger, went forth
with eleven companions to look at the dragon; he had
learned the cause of the feud which so afflicted his
people, for the precious vessel came into his possession
by the hand of the informer. He who had caused the
trouble to begin with, a downcast captive, was the thir-
teenth man in the troop: he had to show them the
place humbly. Against his will, he went to where, as he
knew, the earth hall was. The underground barrow,
full of ornaments and filigreed jewelry, stood near the
rolling sea, the crashing waves. The frightful guardian,
the vigilant fighter, had long held the golden treasure
under the earth—it was not easy for any man to get it.

The warlike king sat on the headland; there the
generous lord of the Geats spoke to his retainers. His
spirit was sad, restless, and ready to depart: near at
hand was the destiny which was about to approach the
old man and seek the treasure of his soul, sunder life
from body. The prince's spirit was not enclosed in flesh
much longer after this.

Beowulf, Ecgtheow's son, spoke: "In youth I sur-
vived many battles and times of war; I remember it all.
I was seven years old when the generous prince, the

friend of the people, received me from my father;
King Hrethel kept and guarded me, gave me wealth
and sustenance, and bore our kinship in mind. I, as a
warrior in the stronghold, was never any less dear to
him than any one of his sons, Herebeald, or Haethcyn,
or my dear Hygelac.

"The deathbed of the eldest was unsuitably spread
for him by a kinsman, for Haethcyn struck down his
brother, his rightful lord, with an arrow from his horn
bow. He missed his mark and hit his kinsman, and
thus one brother killed the other with a bloody shaft.
That was an inexpiable killing: so serious a sin the
thought of it wearies the mind; nevertheless, Herebeald's
death had to go unavenged.

"So it is hard for an old man to endure it when his
young son swings on the gallows; he utters the dirge, a
sorry song, when his son hangs as food for ravens, and
he, though old and wise, cannot give him any help.
Every morning he remembers his son's passing; he
does not wish to wait for another heir in the strong-
hold, when one has experienced the torment of death's
distress. Sorrowful, he sees the deserted wine hall in his
son's dwelling, a windswept resting-place bereft of joy.
The riders sleep, the heroes are in their graves; nor is
there the sound of the harp, or sport in the enclosures,
as there once was. When he takes to his bed, left alone,
he sings a sorrowful song for his son; it seems to him
that the fields and dwellings are all too spacious.

35

"In like manner the protector of the Geats en-
dured overwhelming sorrow in his heart for Herebeald;
there was no way for him to settle the feud with the
murderer, nor could he pursue Haethcyn and punish
him, although he had small love for him. Then, over-
whelmed by his grief, Hrethel gave up the joys of men

and chose the light of God. He left his sons lands and towns, as a prosperous man does, when he departed from life.

"Then there was conflict and warfare between the Swedes and the Geats over the wide water—a bitter feud arose after Hrethel died. Ongentheow's sons were bold and warlike, and they had no wish for peace across the sea, but often carried on terrible attacks near Hreosnabeorh. My kinsmen, Haethcyn and Hygelac, avenged these wicked deeds, as is well known; but it was a hard bargain for one of them since he paid for it with his life. The battle was fatal to Haethcyn, lord of the Geats. Then in the morning, Hygelac saw his brother avenged with the sword by Eofor, who fought with Ongentheow: his war helmet split, the old man of the Swedes fell, pale from battle. Eofor's hand remembered feuds enough: he did not withhold the deadly blow.

"Hygelac gave me land and a splendid dwelling. I repaid him for the treasure he gave me with my bright sword in battle, as it was given me to do. He had no need to seek among the Gifthas or the Danes, or in Sweden, for a lesser warrior to buy with treasure; I would always be in the vanguard of his troop, alone at the front—and I shall do battle always so while this sword endures, the sword which has served me well both before and after the time when I killed Daeghrefn, the champion of the Hugas, in hand-to-hand combat in the presence of the hosts. He could bring no armor as spoils of battle to the Frisian king; for the brave man, the Hugas's standard-bearer, fell in battle. He was not killed by the sword, but my grip stopped the beating of his heart, and broke his body. Now my hand and my strong sword's edge shall fight for the hoard."

Beowulf spoke words of vow for the last time: "I engaged in many battles in youth; now I, as an aged king, shall still seek battle and do glorious deeds, if the wicked ravager will come out of the earth hall to meet me." Then he addressed each of the brave warriors, his dear comrades, for the last time: "I would not use a sword or weapon against the serpent if I knew how else I might grapple mightily with the monster, as I did long ago with Grendel; but I expect hot battle flames, a blast of venomous breath. Therefore I have my shield and coat of mail.

"I will not flee from the barrow's guardian so much as a foot, but what happens to us two at the wall shall be as the Creator of every man allots our destiny. I am so bold in spirit that I need not proclaim vows against this flying monster. Wait on the barrow protected by your mail, men in armor, to see which of us two may better endure wounds after the fatal conflict. It is not your undertaking, nor within any man's power, if not mine alone, to fight against the dragon and win renown. I shall win gold by my valor—or else baleful war shall carry off your lord!"

The famous warrior rose by his shield. Strong in his helmet, he bore his coat of mail under the stone cliffs, trusting in his own single-handed strength: such is not a coward's way. Then the mighty veteran of many battles, who had often been in the thick of the fighting when troops clashed together, saw stone arches standing by the wall, and a stream flowing out there from the barrow. The stream rushed hot with deadly fire, and no one could endure the hollow passage near the hoard for any length of time without being burnt by the dragon's flames.

The stouthearted lord of the Geats called out furiously: his voice penetrated under the gray stone, roaring a clear battle cry. When the guardian of the hoard recognized the man's voice his hatred was aroused—and there was no more time to ask for peace. First the monster's breath came out of the stone, hot battle vapor; the earth resounded. Under the barrow the hero raised his shield against the dreadful stranger, as the coiled

creature's heart was stirred to fight. The good king had
drawn his sword, an ancient heirloom sharp of edge,
and each of the pair of enemies was in horror of the
other.

The warrior stood stouthearted with his high shield;
he waited in his armor while the serpent quickly coiled
himself together: then, the fiery dragon started to glide
in coils, hastening to his destiny. But his shield pro-
tected the glorious lord's life and body for less time
than he wished: there, for the first time, destiny did
not give him triumph in battle. The lord of the Geats
raised his hand up and struck the terrible, many-colored
monster with his ancestral sword, but the blade failed:
the bright steel bit against the bone less strongly than
the king's need dictated. He was oppressed by trouble.

Then the guardian of the hoard, infuriated by the
stroke, cast deadly fire and the hostile flames sprang
everywhere. The king of the Geats could not boast of a
glorious victory, for his naked sword failed in battle,
which no trusty blade should have done. That was no
pleasant journey that Ecgtheow's famous kinsman was
to take, for he must leave this world for another against
his will, as every man must come to the end of his
transitory days.

It was not long before the fighters met again. The
dragon took heart: his breast swelled as he breathed
again—and he who had ruled a nation before was now
in great distress, surrounded by fire. No band of noble
comrades stood courageously about him: they had fled
into the wood to save their lives. But there was one
among them who was deeply grieved. Ties of kinship
can never be put aside by a right-thinking man.

Beowulf's Death

36

This good warrior was a prince of the Swedes
called Wiglaf, son of Weohstan, Aelfhere's kinsman.
When he saw that his lord was suffering from the heat
under his helmet, he remembered the kindnesses
Beowulf had shown to him before—the wealthy dwell-
ing place of the Waegmundings[20] and every share of
the common estate, as his father had had—then he
could not hold back. He seized his yellow linden shield
and drew his ancient sword, which had once belonged
to Eanmund, son of Ohthere.[21]

When Eanmund was a friendless exile, Weohstan
killed him in a sword fight, and bore the shining hel-
met, ringed mail, and ancient giant's sword to Eanmund's
kinsmen. Onela rewarded Weohstan with Eanmund's
armor and war gear—he said nothing of a feud, al-
though Weohstan had killed his brother Ohthere's son.
Weohstan kept the precious trappings for many sea-
sons until his son could accomplish noble deeds like his
old father; then, among the Geats, he gave Wiglaf his
countless battle garments before the old man departed
from life and took his way.

This was the first time that the young champion
was to fight beside his noble lord. His courage did not
dissolve, nor did his father's legacy fail in war; the
serpent found this out when they had met together.

Sad at heart, Wiglaf spoke, saying many words about
duty to his companions: "I remember the time when, as
we drank mead, we promised the lord who gave us
treasure in the beer hall that we would repay him for

---

[20]The family to which Beowulf and Wiglaf belong.
[21]See note 19, p. 62.

that war gear, helmets, and hard swords, if such a need befell him. Then he chose us out of the host for this expedition of his own will: he considered us worthy of glory, and gave me these treasures, because he considered us good warriors, keen helmet-wearers—although our lord intended to carry out this valorous work alone, since he has done more glorious deeds and daring acts than anyone else.

"Now the day has come when our leader needs the support of mighty warriors. Let us go to him and help our war chief, as long as the heat of the grim fire-terror shall last! God knows that for my part I would much rather the flame swallowed up my body together with my lord. It does not seem right to me that we should bear our shields back home unless we may first kill the foe, and defend the life of the lord of the Geats. I know well that this is not what he deserves for his former deeds: that he alone of the Geat veterans should suffer harm and sink in battle; we shall share sword and helmet, mail and battle garb."

Then he advanced through the deadly fumes, bearing a shield to help his lord and saying: "Dear Beowulf, carry out all things well! You said in your youthful days that you would never let your fame decline as long as you live; now, resolute prince, famous for your deeds, you must defend your life with all your might. I shall help you!"

Hearing this, the dragon came back furiously; the horrible, malicious foe, bright with streaming fire, returned once more to attack his enemies, the hated men. Waves of fire advanced toward them. The linden shield burnt to the rim, and the young warrior's mail could give him no help: but when his own was destroyed by flames, the youth boldly went under his kinsman's shield. The warlike king was still intent on glory, and he struck with his sword, using such great strength that it drove into the dragon's head. But the force of the blow completely shattered Beowulf's sword, Naegling; the bright heirloom failed in battle. It was not granted to him that any sword could help him in battle, for his hand was too strong. I have heard that his stroke overtaxed every sword; no matter how hard a weapon he bore to battle, it did not help him at all.

Now the enemy of men made up his mind to fight for the third time; the terrible, fiery dragon rushed at the hero when it saw its chance. The red-hot ferocious beast encircled Beowulf's neck with its bitter tusks, bathing him in his life's blood; blood flowed in streams.

37

But then, I have heard, in this moment of need, the noble warrior at the king's side showed his valor, the skill and boldness which was his nature. The brave man paid no attention to the dragon's head, although his hand burned as he helped his kinsman, and he struck the hostile creature lower down; the shining sword sank in so that the fire began to die down at once. Now the king himself collected his wits and drew the deadly knife, keen and battle sharp, which he wore on his armor; the protector of the Geats slashed through the serpent in the middle. They had felled the enemy— valor had driven out its life, and the two kindred noblemen had killed it. This is what a man should be, a thane in time of need! That was to be the king's last victory, the last of this world's work that he would do.

For the wound which the earth dragon had inflicted on him before began to burn and swell, and he soon found that deadly poison raged within his body. The thoughtful prince went to sit on a seat by the wall; he looked on that work of giants and saw how the ancient barrow had stone arches within it, fast on pillars. His good thane took water in his hands and washed

the bloodstained lord; he cared for his friend and ruler,
wearied with battle, and unfastened his helmet.

Beowulf spoke, in spite of his deadly wounds—he
knew well that he had reached the end of his allotted
days of earthly joy; all his time was gone, death immea-
surably near. He said, "Now I would have wished to
give my armor to my son, if I had been granted an heir
of the body to succeed me. I ruled the people fifty
winters, and there was no king in any of the neighbor-
ing countries who dared to approach me with warriors
and threaten me with terror. In my home I awaited my
fate, kept what was my own well, and did not seek
treacherous quarrels, nor swear false oaths. Though I
suffer with fatal wounds, I may take joy in all that,
since the Ruler of men need not lay the murder of
kinsmen to my charge when my life leaves my body.

"Now go quickly, dear Wiglaf, to look at the hoard
under the gray stone, since the serpent lies dead; now
he sleeps sorely wounded, bereft of treasure. Make
haste, so that I may look at the ancient wealth, the
golden treasure, and clearly see the curious bright gems;
then I may with greater comfort because of the wealth
of treasure give up my life and the country I have long
ruled."

38

Then, I heard, Weohstan's son quickly obeyed the
words of his wounded lord. In his ring-mail he went
under the roof of the barrow. When the brave young
retainer, exulting in victory, went by the seat there, he
saw glittering gold and many precious jewels lying on
the ground, wonders on the wall, and the den of the
serpent, the old night-flyer; he saw cups, the vessels of
men of old, standing there without a polisher and de-
prived of ornaments. There was many an old and rusty
helmet and many skillfully twisted arm-rings.—Treasure,

gold in the ground, can easily overpower any man, hide it who will.—Likewise he saw a golden standard hanging high over the hoard, the greatest of wonders woven by skillful hands; from this a light arose, so that he could perceive the surface of the floor and look over the ornaments. There was nothing to be seen of the serpent, for the sword's edge had carried him off.

Then, I heard, the hoard of old giants' work in the barrow was plundered by a man; he loaded cups and dishes in his bosom at his own will and also took the standard, brightest of emblems. The old lord's iron-edged sword had already killed the creature who had so long guarded the treasure, waging war in the middle of the night with fierce, terrible, burning flames for the sake of the hoard, until he was killed.

Moved by the hoard, the messenger was eager to hasten back, anxiously wondering whether he would find the lord of the Geats alive there where he had left him, deprived of strength. Returning with the treasure he found the glorious prince his lord, bleeding, his life at an end; he began to throw water on him again, until words began to escape him.

The suffering old king looked at the gold and said: "I give thanks to the Lord—to the King of glory, the eternal Ruler—for all the treasures that I now gaze on; I give thanks that I could gain such for my people before my death-day. Now I have sold my old lifespan for the hoard of treasure; now you must take care of the people's needs. I cannot be here longer. After I have been burned on the fire, have the warriors raise a splendid mound at the promontory of the sea; it shall be a remembrance to my people towering high on Hronesness, so that afterwards the seafarers who drive ships far over the dusky sea will call it Beowulf's barrow."

The valiant lord undid the golden collar from his neck and gave it to the young warrior, along with his golden helmet, ring, and coat of mail, and bade him to

use them well: "You are the last of our kin, the
Waegmundings; fate has swept away all my kinsmen,
the valorous noblemen, to their destiny. I shall follow
them."

These were the last words the old man spoke be-
fore he was ready for the hot, hostile flames of his
funeral pyre. His soul departed to seek the judgment
of the righteous.

Tidings and Prophecies

39

It was a sad moment for the younger man when he
saw his dear lord lying wretched on the ground, his
life at an end. His slayer also lay dead; the terrible
dragon had been overcome and destroyed. No longer
could the coiled serpent keep watch over the treasure
hoard, for the hammer-sharpened war sword had car-
ried it off and the winged beast fell on the ground near
the treasure house, stilled by its wounds. Never again
did it fly through the air and appear in the middle of
the night, proud of its precious property: it fell to the
earth, killed by the hand of the warrior. Indeed, I have
heard that no man of might, no matter how daring,
could successfully rush against the breath of the ven-
omous foe, or disturb the hoard of rings with his hands,
if he found the guardian awake in the barrow. Beowulf
paid for that princely treasure with death; he and the
dragon had both come to the end of their mortal life.

It was not long after this that the cowards came out
of the wood: ten craven traitors together, who had not
dared to use their javelins in their lord's great need.
Shamefaced, they came with their shields and battle
garments to the place where the old man lay and gazed
at Wiglaf, who was sitting wearily near the shoulder of
his lord, trying to rouse his king with water. But he did

not succeed at all. No matter how much he wished it, he could not keep the chieftain alive on earth, nor turn aside the Ruler's decree; God's judgment ruled over every man, as it still does now.

Now those whose courage had failed did not have to wait long for a grim rebuke from the young champion. Wiglaf, Weohstan's son, looked at them with dislike; sick at heart, he said, "So: a man who wants to tell the truth can say that the king who gave you the treasures and warlike equipment that you stand in there—when over the ale-bench that lord gave the most splendid helmets and coats of mail that he could find, far and near, to his retainers in the hall—he completely threw away the war gear—to his sorrow. When war came upon him, the king had no need to boast of his comrades in battle. Nevertheless, God, the Ruler of victories, allowed him to avenge himself single-handed with his sword when he had need of courage. I could not give him much protection in battle, but I gave my kinsman what little help I could. The deadly foe weakened when I struck it with my sword: fire streamed less swiftly from its head.

"Too few defenders thronged around the prince when distress came upon him. Now the receiving of treasure and giving of swords, all the enjoyment of hereditary estate and comfort, shall cease for you and your kin; every man of your clan will have to turn away, deprived of the landowner's privileges, when noblemen far and wide hear of your flight, your shameful act. Death is better to every noble warrior than life in disgrace!"

40

Then he ordered the events of the battle to be announced in the stronghold up over the sea cliff, where the noblemen of the court had been sitting

mournfully all through the morning; the warriors did
not know whether to expect the death or the return of
their dear lord. The messenger who rode along the
headland did not keep back the tiding, but said truth-
fully in the hearing of all, "Now the dear king of our
people is fast on his deathbed; the lord of the Geats lies
slaughtered by the dragon. His deadly enemy lies be-
side him, killed by knife wounds: he could not wound
the monster with a sword at all. Wiglaf, son of Weohstan,
sits by Beowulf, watching over his dead kinsman. Griev-
ing, the nobleman holds his vigil over both friend and
foe.

"Now the people must expect a time of strife, once
the fall of the king becomes widely known among the
Franks and the Frisians. Hard fighting was launched
against the Hugas when Hygelac went with a sea army
into the Frisian land, where the Hetwares assailed him
in battles. With courage and superior strength, they
brought about the fall of that mailed warrior; Hygelac
fell among his troops. No more did the chieftain give
prizes to his veterans. Since then the king of the Frisians
has felt no kindness to us.

"Nor do I expect any peace or faith at all from the
Swedish people, for it is widely known that Ongentheow[22]
killed Haethcyn, son of Hrethel, near Ravenswood,
where the Geatish people first arrogantly attacked the
Swedes. Ohthere's father, old and terrible, soon repaid
Haethcyn for his attack: he cut down that sea leader
and rescued his own wife, the aged mother of Onela and
Ohthere, bereft of her gold ornaments; and then he so
pursued his deadly foes that they barely escaped, lord-
less, into Ravenswood. There with a large army he
besieged the survivors, who were weary with wounds.
All night long he threatened the unhappy band with
destruction and said he would kill them with the sword

---

[22]A Swedish king, father of Ohthere and Onela.

in the morning, and put some on the gallows tree as a
sport for the birds. With daybreak help came to the
wretched men when they heard the sound of Hygelac's
horn and trumpet, as the good man came after them
with a host of tried warriors.

41

"The bloody trail of Swedes and Geats, how the
people fought together in a gory conflict, was widely
evident. Then the aged chieftain, sad at heart, went
with his kinsmen to seek his fastness: King Ongentheow
withdrew, for he had heard of Hygelac's fighting skill
and he did not expect that he could resist the proud
warrior's craft and fight against the seamen to defend
his treasure, and the women and children, against the
raiders. So he turned away again; the old man went
behind an earth-wall. The Swedish people were given
pursuit; Hygelac's standard went forth over the field of
refuge until the Geats thronged about the enclosure.

"There gray-haired Ongentheow was brought
to bay at sword's point, and the king was at Eofor's[23]
mercy. Angrily, Wulf, son of Wonred, struck at Ongen-
theow with his weapon—because of that stroke his blood
sprang forth under his hair in streams. But the old
king of the Swedes was not afraid; he quickly turned
and paid back the deadly blow with a worse one. Now
Wonred's son could not give a return blow to the old
warrior, for Ongentheow cut through the helmet on
his head first, so that he sank down stained with blood.
He fell on the ground, but he was not yet doomed; he
recovered, although the wound hurt him. When his
brother lay wounded, Hygelac's thane, Eofor, with his
heirloom sword broke through the protecting shield-
wall to the giant helmet. Then the king fell: the peo-

---

[23]A Geat warrior; brother of Wulf, son of Wonred—cf. p. 65.

ple's guardian was mortally wounded. Many men bound up the wounds of Eofor's kinsman and quickly raised him up, now that it was their fortune to rule the battle-field. Meanwhile Eofor rifled Ongentheow and took his iron mail, and his strong hilted sword and helmet too; he bore the gray-haired king's armor to Hygelac, who received the ornaments and made him an honorable promise of rewards among the people—and he fulfilled it well.

"When Hrethel's son, lord of the Geats, had returned home, he repaid Eofor and Wulf for the battle with vast treasure: he gave each of them a hundred thousand units of land and linked rings. No man on earth had cause to blame him for the reward, since they had earned it for brave deeds. And then Hygelac gave Eofor his only daughter in marriage to grace his home, as a pledge of favor.

"That is the feud and enmity, mortal hatred between men, for which I expect that the people of the Swedes will attack us when they hear of the death of our lord, who previously guarded our treasure and kingdom against enemies; after the fall of other heroes, bold Scyldings, he helped the people and performed noble deeds.

"Now it would be best if we hastened to look at the king there, and bring to the funeral pyre him who gave us treasure. Nor shall only a part of the treasure hoard melt with the brave hero; that vast amount of gold, so grimly purchased, rings bought in the end with his own life: these the fire shall eat, the flames enfold. No nobleman shall wear an ornament as a remembrance, nor shall a lovely maiden have a necklace around her throat—sad of heart and bereft of gold, they shall tread a foreign country, not once, but many times, now that the leader of the army has laid aside laughter, joy, and mirth. Therefore many a morning-cold spear shall be gripped and lifted in men's hands; no more shall the sound of the harp wake the warriors; but the dark raven, eager for the doomed, shall have much to say and tell the eagle how he fared at the meal when he rifled the dead with the wolf."

Thus the warrior told the unwelcome message; he did not lie as to events or words. The band rose up; all unhappy, with tears flowing, they went under Earnaness to see the wondrous sight. There they found him who gave them rings in former times lying on the sand, on his bed of rest; there the hero's last day had passed, the day in which the warlike king of the Geats died a wondrous death.

First they saw a stranger being there—the hateful serpent, lying opposite on the field; the fiery dragon, terrible in its coloring, was scorched with flames. It was fifty feet long in the place where it lay. Before, it had kept to the joyous air at night, then swooped downward to seek out its den; now it was still in death. It had made its last use of barrows. By the dragon stood cups and pitchers; dishes and precious swords lay there, rusty and eaten through, since they had lain there within the bosom of the earth a thousand winters.

Moreover, that huge heritage, the gold of men of old, had been bound with a spell so that no man could touch the ring hall—unless God himself, true King of victories (he is man's protection) granted to whom he would to open the hoard: even to whichever man seemed meet to him.

Beowulf's Funeral

42

It was clear now that the creature who had wrongly kept guard over the treasure in the wall had not prospered in his course. That guardian first killed a man with few peers, but that attack was severely avenged.

No one knows where a famous hero may reach the end of his life, or when a man may no longer dwell with his kinsmen in the mead-hall. Thus it was for Beowulf when he sought battle with the barrow's guardian; he himself did not know what would bring about his parting from the world. The glorious chieftains who put the treasure there to stay until Doomsday made so solemn an oath that the man who plundered the place would be guilty of sin and confined to places of heathen damnation, held fast by hell-bonds and grievously tormented—unless he had first seen the gold-bestowing grace of the Almighty.

Wiglaf, son of Weohstan, spoke: "For one nobleman's sake, many others must often endure misery, as has happened to us. We could not advise the dear lord or counsel the king not to approach the guardian of the gold, but to let it lie where it had long been and inhabit its dwelling until the end of the world; he held to his high destiny. The hoard, grimly obtained, is opened to view; that destiny which impelled the king here was too strong.

"I entered the barrow, and looked all around it, saw the precious objects of the building, when my way was clear: I had no friendly welcome to come in under the earth-wall. Hastily I seized a great burden of hoarded treasures in my hands and bore it back to my king.

"He was still alive, sound in mind and conscious. The old man said much in his suffering; he bade me greet you, and tell you to make a high barrow on the site of his funeral pyre: a great and glorious monument your lord deserved for his deeds, for when he was alive he was the most worthy warrior anywhere on earth. Now let us hurry and see the heap of curious gems again, the wonder under the wall; I will show you the way, so that you will see the rings and broad gold closely enough. Let the bier be prepared and quickly made ready when we come out; and there we shall

79

carry our lord, the beloved man, to the place where he shall long abide in the keeping of the Almighty."

Then Wiglaf, Weohstan's brave son, gave orders that many houseowners be told to bring firewood from afar for the good lord: "Now the flame shall grow murky and the fire consume the ruler of warriors, who so often withstood the shower of iron when the storm of arrows, driven by the bowstrings, shook over the shield-wall, and the feathered shaft did its duty and sped the barb."

Next Weohstan's son summoned together seven of the best of the king's band of retainers, and went under the enemy's roof with seven warriors; he who went at the head bore a torch in his hand. It was not decided by lot who plundered that hoard: when the men saw any part remain in the room without a guardian, lying forsaken, little did any hesitate to carry out the precious treasures hastily. They shoved the dragon over the cliff and let the waves take the guardian of the treasure, the flood embrace it. Then a vast amount of twisted gold of every kind was loaded on the wagon, and the noble gray-haired warrior was borne to Hronesness.

The people of the Geats prepared him a magnificent pyre on the ground, hung about with helmets, battle shields, and bright coats of mail, as he had requested. Then the lamenting warriors laid their glorious leader in the midst, and began to wake the greatest of funeral fires on the barrow. Wood smoke climbed up, dark over the flames; roaring fire mingled with weeping—the tumult of the wind subsided—until the fire had crumbled the body, hot to the heart. Sadly they complained of their distress, mourning the death of their ruler; and a Geatish woman, with hair bound up, sorrowfully sang a sad lament for Beowulf, saying that she dreaded evil days of mourning, filled with great slaughter, terror of the enemy, harm and captivity. Heaven swallowed the smoke.

Then the Geatish people made a shelter on the promontory. It was high and broad, widely visible to seafarers; in ten days they finished building the famous warrior's beacon. Around the leavings of the fire they made the best wall skilled men could devise. In the barrow they put rings and jewels and all such adornments that warlike men had taken from the hoard; they left the noble treasure for the earth to hold, buried the gold in the soil, where it still lies now, as useless to men as before.

Twelve brave warriors, sons of princes, rode around the fire to express their sorrow and to lament the king. They composed an elegy about the hero, praising his nobility and extolling his deeds of valor, for it is meet that a man should praise his lord in words and love him in his heart, when his spirit leaves his body.

Thus the people of the Geats mourned their lord's fall. They said that among the world's kings, he was the mildest and gentlest of men, most kind to his people and most eager for praise.

Other Poems

Other Poems

Deor

Weland,[1] sorely hindered, knew wretchedness: the steadfast nobleman suffered misfortune—sorrow and longing were his only comrades. Misery was his lot, wretched as the cold of winter, when Nithhad constrained him, laying bonds of supple sinew on the better man. That passed by; this can, too.

In Beadohild's breast her brother's death was not so sore a weight as her own condition, when she could clearly see that she grew great with child. Nor could she consider with unflinching mind what was to come of that. That passed by; this can, too.

We have heard of the moans of Geat's lady, Mathhild,[2] which grew so boundless that her love and sorrow drove away all sleep. That passed by; this can, too.

---

[1] The legendary Germanic smith. King Nithhad, coveting his work, imprisoned him; some versions say he hamstrung Weland, which may explain the "bonds of supple sinew." Weland took vengeance by killing Nithhad's sons (and presenting the king with artifacts made of their skulls and teeth) and seducing his daughter Beadohild, then escaped with the aid of wings (like Daedalus) leaving Beadohild pregnant. However, after Nithhad died of chagrin, Weland took Beadohild as his wife. Their son became a famous hero.

[2] This may refer to the story of a bride who foresaw that she would drown on her wedding journey; one version of this tale says that her husband, "Geat," was able to rescue her. In any case, the story concerns the sorrows of a woman in circumstances obviously different from those of Beadohild.

For thirty years Theodoric[3] held the stronghold of the Merings: that was known to many. That passed by; this can, too.

We have learned of Ermanaric's[4] wolfish mind. He held the broad realm of the Gothic people: that was a grim king! Many a man sat bound in sorrow, expecting yet more misery, continually wishing that kingdom overthrown. That passed by; this can, too.

When a man sits sorrowful, cut off from all pleasure, dark gloom in his breast, his measure of misfortune seeming never ending: he may then consider that throughout this world the omniscient Lord[5] continually turns about, alloting many a nobleman grace and assured glory, and others a measure of misery. That which I would say about myself is that I was once the minstrel of the Hedenings, dear to their lord. Deor was my name. For many years I held that honorable office and had a gracious lord, until now Heorrenda, a man skilled in song, has been granted the land which the nobleman's protector had given me before. That passed by;[6] this can, too.

---

[3]Either a Frankish king of the early sixth century (or his legendary son) or the great Ostrogoth of the same period, known to the Anglo-Saxons as the persecutor and slayer of Boethius, Symmachus, and Pope John. If the latter is meant, "that was known to many" is an example of the ironic litotes which is a frequent effect in Old English poetry: Boethius, for example, certainly knew of Theodoric's tyranny.

[4]Historical king of the Ostrogoths (d. ca. 375); in Germanic narrative, he often (but not always) appears as a bloodthirsty tyrant.

[5]Capitalization of "lord" is, of course, editorial; the phrase is open to interpretation. For example, the "lord" referred to could also be a terrestrial ruler, such as the one Deor served (referred to a few lines further on), who also turned his favor first to one man, then to another.

[6]In the earlier stanzas, this refrain refers to the passing of hard times in stories which ended happily: "that" refers to the hardships endured by Weland, Beadohild, etc., and "this" to the speaker's own hardships, i.e., the loss of the favor of the (legendary) lord of the Hedenings. The last line also suggests that the speaker's difficulties will pass, but apparently with a change of reference: here, "that" seems to refer to the *good* times which have passed; hence, he concludes, since God continually changes the world, his bad times ("this") will also come to an end.

Caedmon's Hymn[1]

Now let us praise the Guardian of heaven, the might of the Maker and his mind and thought, as the eternal Lord arranged the beginning of all things wonderful.

First he created the heavens as a roof for the children of men, holy Creator; then mankind's Guardian fashioned earth afterwards, the eternal Lord: he made the land for man—almighty God!

---

[1]For an account of the composition of this poem, in the middle of the seventh century, see Bede's *Ecclesiastical History of England* (completed ca. 731), Book IV, Chapter 24. —Readers of *Beowulf* may find it interesting to compare this lyrical description of creation with the scop's song of creation in Heorot in the beginning of Part I.

The Battle of Brunanburh

In this year[1] King Athelstan, lord of noblemen generous to warriors, and his brother, Prince Edmund, with him, won eternal glory with their swords in battle around Brunanburh. The sons of Edward cleft through the shield-wall and hewed the solid shields with their well-forged blades. Such was their nature and their heritage always to defend their land, its treasures and its homes, in battle with each enemy. The invaders perished; Scotsmen and vikings fell down doomed. The field was overflown with the blood of men since first the sun, God's bright candle, rose up in the morning over the ground until that glorious planet, noble creation of the eternal Lord, sank to its seat. Many a warrior lay there, drained of life by the pointed spears: Norsemen shot down over their shields, and Scots, spent, sated with war.

The West Saxons swept forward all day long, close on the tracks of the hated foe, sternly cutting down fleeing warriors from behind. The Mercians did not refuse hard hand-combat to any of the company which

---

[1]937; the poem, recording an historic battle, appears in the Anglo-Saxon Chronicle for this year. Athelstan (grandson of Alfred), king of the West Saxons, and his brother led the English to an important victory over an invading army of Norse vikings (led by Olaf) and Scots (led by King Constantine). The exact location of Brunanburh is not known, however.

came with Olaf, those who crossed the sea and sought out the land, fated to die in battle. Five young kings lay on the field of war; the sword put them to sleep, and likewise seven of Olaf's own noblemen, with a countless host of the vikings and the Scots.

The chief of the Norsemen was there put to flight. Compelled by necessity, he boarded his ship with a greatly dwindled host. The ship pressed out to sea and the king sailed away over the dark waters, escaping with his life. There also was the old campaigner driven in retreat: gray-haired Constantine fled to his northern home. He had no need to rejoice when sword met sword in battle. Bereft of kinsmen, his friends felled on the meeting-ground, slain in the battle, he had to leave his son in the place of slaughter, the young man destroyed by wounds of war. The wily old gray-beard had no cause to boast over what the sword cut down—and no more did Olaf. With the remnants of their army, they did not need to exult that they had had the better on the battlefield when banners clashed in the exchange of blows when men's spears met on the field of slaughter when they were matched against the sons of Edward.

The Norsemen departed in their nailed ships, downcast survivors of the flight of spears; seeking for Dublin, they sailed the deep waters, coming back to Ireland dejected and ashamed. Like them,[2] both the brothers— king and prince—sought their home, the land of the West Saxons, exulting in the outcome of the war. They left behind them, dividing up the corpses, dark-coated scavengers, the horny-beaked black raven and the eagle with its dusky coat, white in back, to enjoy the carrion with the greedy war hawk and the wild gray creature, the wolf of the forest.

Never was there greater slaughter on this island, so many men cut down by the sword, before this, as the

---

[2]Implying, of course, how very *unlike* this homecoming was.

books tell us—written by wise men in the days of old—
since Angles and Saxons made their way here from the
east, seeking Britain over the broad sea, when the keen
warriors overcame the Welshmen, and the glorious
noblemen won their homeland.

The Battle of Brunanburh

Translated by Alfred Lord Tennyson

I

Athelstan King,
Lord among Earls,
Bracelet-bestower and
Baron of Barons,
He with his brother,
Edmund Atheling,
Gaining a lifelong
Glory in battle,
Slew with the sword-edge
There by Brunanburh,
Brake the shield-wall,
Hewed the lindenwood,
Hacked the battleshield,
Sons of Edward with hammered brands.

II

Theirs was a greatness
Got from their Grandsires—
Theirs that so often in
Strife with their enemies
Struck for their hoards and their hearths and their homes.

III

Bowed the spoiler,
Bent the Scotsman,
Fell the shipcrews
Doomed to the death.
All the field with blood of the fighters
Flowed, from when first the great
Sun-star of morningtide,
Lamp of the Lord God
Lord everlasting,
Glode over earth till the glorious creature
Sank to his setting.

IV

There lay many a man
Marred by the javelin,
Men of the Northland
Shot over shield.
There was the Scotsman
Weary of war.

V

We the West-Saxons,
Long as the daylight
Lasted, in companies
Troubled the track of the host that we hated,
Grimly with swords that were sharp from the
grindstone,
Fiercely we hacked at the flyers before us.

VI

Mighty the Mercian,
Hard was his hand-play,
Sparing not any of
Those that with Anlaf,
Warriors over the

Weltering waters
Borne in the bark's-bosom,
Drew to this island:
Doomed to the death.

VII

Five young kings put asleep by the sword-stroke,
Seven strong Earls of the army of Anlaf
Fell on the war-field, numberless numbers,
Shipmen and Scotsmen.

VIII

Then the Norse leader,
Dire was his need of it,
Few were his following,
Fled to his warship:
Fleeted his vessel to sea with the king in it,
Saving his life on the fallow flood.

IX

Also the crafty one,
Constantinus,
Crept to his North again,
Hoar-headed hero!

X

Slender warrant had
He to be proud of
The welcome of war-knives—
He that was reft of his
Folk and his friends that had
Fallen in conflict,
Leaving his son too
Lost in the carnage,
Mangled to morsels,
A youngster in war!

XI

Slender reason had
He to be glad of
The clash of the war-glaive—
Traitor and trickster
And spurner of treaties—
He nor had Anlaf
With armies so broken
A reason for bragging
That they had the better
In perils of battle
On places of slaughter—
The struggle of standards,
The rush of the javelins,
The crash of the charges,
The wielding of weapons—
The play that they played with
The children of Edward.

XII

Then with their nailed prows
Parted the Norsemen, a
Blood-reddened relic of
Javelins over
The jarring breaker, the deep-sea billow,
Shaping their way toward Dyflen again,
Shamed in their souls.

XIII

Also the brethren,
King and Atheling,
Each in his glory,
Went to his own in his own West-Saxonland,
Glad of the war.

XIV

Many a carcase they left to be carrion,
Many a livid one, many a sallow-skin—
Left for the white tailed eagle to tear it, and
Left for the horny-nibbed raven to rend it, and
Gave to the garbaging war-hawk to gorge it, and
That gray beast, the wolf of the weald.

XV

Never had huger
Slaughter of heroes
Slain by the sword-edge—
Such as old writers
Have writ of in histories—
Hapt in this isle, since
Up from the East hither
Saxon and Angle from
Over the broad billow
Broke into Britain with
Haughty war-workers who
Harried the Welshman, when
Earls that were lured by the
Hunger of glory gat
Hold of the land.

The Dream of the Rood

Listen, and I will tell you the very best of dreams
which came to me in the middle of the night, while the
tongues of men remained at rest. It seemed to me that
I saw an extraordinary tree, brightest of all beams,
towering up into the air and wound about with light.
That beacon was all covered with gold and lovely gems:
some stood at its base, fair on the surface of the earth,
and five more gleamed above up on the crossbeam.
Hosts of angels, eternally fair, kept watch over it. This
was no gallows for a common criminal. Holy spirits
watched it, men all over the earth and all this glorious
creation.

Strange and rare was that triumphant tree, while I,
stained by sins, was torn by my faults. I saw the tree of
glory in honorable attire, shining, beautiful, arrayed
with gold: the Ruler's tree was honorably covered with
gems. Yet, through that gold, I could still see an earlier
wretched ordeal, for it began to shed blood on the
right side. I was terribly troubled with grief, afraid
because of that fair vision. I saw that quick beacon
change attire and color: sometimes it was drenched with
moisture, covered with the flow of blood, sometimes
arrayed with treasure.

But as I lay there for a long time, sadly I watched

the Savior's tree—until I heard it call out, and the best of all wood spoke these words:

"It was long ago—well I remember!—when I was cut down at the edge of the forest and taken from my trunk. Strong enemies took me there and made a spectacle of me, ordering me to lift up their criminals. Men bore me on their shoulders there until they set me up on a hill; enemies enough fastened me firmly there. Then I saw mankind's Lord hastening and full of zeal: he wished to mount upon me. I did not dare to break or bend against the Lord's command when I saw the trembling of the surface of the earth. I could have dashed down all the enemies, but I stood fast.

"The young Hero—who was God almighty—stripped off his attire; strong and resolute, he mounted the high gallows, brave in the sight of many when he wished to free mankind. I trembled when the Warrior embraced me; however, I did not dare to bow to the earth or fall down to the surface of the ground. I had to stand fast. I was raised up as the rood; I lifted up the powerful King, Lord of heaven, and I did not dare bow down.

"They drove through me with dark nails: the wounds are still visible, open signs of malice. Yet I dared not harm any of them. They mocked us both together. I was terribly drenched with blood, flowing from the Man's side when he yielded up his spirit. Many cruel blows of fate I endured on that hill! I saw the God of hosts grievously stretched out. Darkness had covered the Ruler's corpse with clouds; over that bright radiance there came forth shadow, dark beneath the clouds. All creation wept, lamenting the King's fall. Christ was on the rood.

"But now quick men came from afar, hastening to the Prince. I watched all that. I was sorely troubled with grief, but I bowed down to the warriors' hands, humbly, full of zeal. There they took almighty God, lifting him up from the heavy torment. The warriors left me standing there, covered with blood: I was terribly torn with iron points. They laid the weary Warrior down and stood by the head of his body. There they watched the Lord of heaven, and he rested there for a while, exhausted by the great ordeal. They began to make a sepulcher for him—warriors still within view of his bane—[1] carving it out of bright stone, and in that they set the Ruler of triumphs. When they were ready to depart, exhausted, from the glorious Lord, they raised a song of sorrow, wretched in the evening-time: he rested there, with little company.

"We[2] still stood there, weeping in that place for a long time. The voices of the warriors faded away. The body grew cold, fair dwelling of the soul. Then someone came to fell us all to the ground: that was a frightful fate! Someone buried us deep in a pit. But the Lord's friends and servants[3] found me there and arrayed me with silver and gold.

"Now, my dear friend, you must understand that I have endured the work of evildoers and suffered sore grief. Now the time has come when I am honored far and wide by men all over the earth and all this glorious creation prays to this beacon. On me God's Son suffered for a while: therefore I now rise up glorious under heaven, and I can save every one of those who hold me in awe. Once I became the hardest of torments, most hateful to the people, before I opened up the right way of life for men of all tongues. Behold: the Father of glory, Guardian of heaven, then honored me above all wood of the forest, just as the almighty God honored his mother, Mary, over all womankind, for all men's sake.

"Now, my dear friend, I bid you to tell this vision

---

[1] Probably refers to the Cross, as unwilling instrument of Christ's death.

[2] The three crosses (though the other two are not mentioned before, they are clearly included in the following lines).

[3] A reference to St. Helena and the Invention (finding) of the True Cross.

to men, revealing in words that this is the tree of glory
on which almighty God suffered for mankind's many
sins and Adam's deeds of old. He tasted death there:
nonetheless, after that the Lord arose in his great might
to be of help to men. He ascended into heaven then,
but he shall return to earth again on Doomsday, the
Lord himself to seek out mankind. Almighty God shall
come with his angels, and he who is Judge over all shall
give judgment to each of them according to what he
has earned here in this transitory life. None can then
be unafraid of the words the Ruler speaks, for he
shall ask the many where that man is who for the
Lord's name would taste bitter death, as he did before
on the beam that is the Cross. And they shall be afraid
then, and think of little which they can say to Christ.
Yet neither need any man be afraid there who bears in
his heart the best of all beacons, for through the rood
shall every soul seek the kingdom from his earthly
path, if he wants to remain with the Ruler."

Then, in joyful mood and full of zeal, I made my
prayer to that beam, alone as I was with little company.
Urged by my heart to go quickly forth on the way,[4] I
endured a time of great longing. Now it is my life's joy
to seek alone for that triumphant beam, to honor it
more often than other men do: my desire for it is much
in my mind and I look for my protection from the
rood. I have few powerful friends in this world; they
have all departed, leaving worldly joys behind. They
sought the King of glory and now they live in heaven,
remaining in glory with the Father of all. Every day I
expect the rood of the Lord, which I saw before here on
this earth, to fetch me away from this transitory life and
bring me where true bliss is, and joy in heaven, where
the Lord's people sit at the feast and bliss is everlasting,

[4]I.e., "the right way of life," the way to heaven, which the Cross has just
explained that it "opened."

and set me there where for ever after I may remain in glory and fully share in the joys of the saints.

May the Lord befriend me, he who once on earth suffered on the gallows-tree for the sins of man. He then freed us, and gave us life in a heavenly home. Joy was restored, and abundant bliss, for those who had endured the fires of hell. The Son was triumphant, mighty in battle, when he returned with those many—a great host of spirits—into God's kingdom, almighty Ruler: to the joy of angels and of all the saints who had remained before in glory in heaven, the Lord, the almighty God, came into his own realm.

The Wanderer

"Often the lone man may abide grace, the mercy of the Maker, though he may have long had to labor with his hands steering a course across the frosty sea, with a mind full of care—following the paths of exile over watery ways. Destiny cannot be changed," the Wanderer reflected, recalling times of wretchedness, deadly combats, and the fall of friends and family.

"Often I have had to bewail my cares alone at each day's dawn. There is no one now alive to whom I dare confide the thoughts of my inmost mind. I know, indeed, that it is a noble custom for a well-bred man to bind his thoughts up firmly deep within his breast, to keep his heart to himself no matter what he thinks. A disheartened mind cannot alter destiny, nor can bitter thoughts bring about help. As men who would earn favor often bind within their breasts all their dreary thoughts, so I have had to enclose my heart in fetters, often afflicted with wretched cares, cut off from native land and far from noble kindred since the time, long ago, when I covered my lord with the darkness of earth and steered my course from there, oppressed with wintry cares, over the ice-bound waves.

"Deprived of a mead-hall, I drearily sought for a generous patron, seeking a hall where, either near or far, I might find one to understand my thoughts and comfort me, a friendless man, with joyous entertainment. He who has tried it knows how cruel a comrade sorrow is to one who has few beloved friends. The paths of exile occupy him, not golden ornaments; a breast full of cold grief, not earthly wealth. He remembers comrades in the hall and the treasure he received and how his patron entertained him at the feast in the days of his youth. But all joy fell away. He knows this certainly who must long forgo his dear lord's words of counsel.

"When sleep and sorrow together bind the lone man in his wretchedness, to his mind it often seems that he embraces his lord, laying hands and head on his knee in homage as he used to do in former days when he enjoyed the bounty of the throne: but then the friendless man wakes up again and sees before him nothing but dark waves, and the seabirds bathing, spreading out their feathers, with frost and snow falling, mingled with hail. Then the heart's wounds are all the heavier, sore with longing for the dear one. Sorrow is redoubled when the mind turns to the memory of kinsmen, gladly greeting them and eagerly beholding them. His companions[1] swim away again. Those floating ones bring no familiar words there to one who must often send his weary heart over the ice-bound waves with redoubled cares.

"Thus I can see no reason in the world why my mind should not darken when I consider every aspect of the lives of warriors and how suddenly the brave young retainers left the hall-floor: every day this Middle-Earth falters and falls away. A man cannot become wise until he has spent many winters in this world. A wise man must be patient: not too hot of temper or too hasty in speech, neither too soft a man nor too reckless,

---

[1] I take these "companions" to be the seabirds, as above, and as ironically intended: compare the personification of "sorrow" as a "cruel comrade" earlier.

too fearful, or too willing, nor too greedy for reward, nor too quick in making vows before he knows he can fulfill them. A stout-hearted warrior should wait to make his vows until he knows exactly where his heart's thoughts may turn.

"The clear-sighted man will know how terrible it will be when all the wealth of this world stands waste, as now in many places everywhere on earth there stand walls beaten by the wind and covered with frost, snow-swept buildings. The wine-hall falls in ruins and its ruler lies cut off from joy; the band of proud retainers has all fallen by the wall. War took off some, sweeping them away; this one was carried over the high seas by a bird of prey, and the gray wolf shared another one with death; that one was buried in a grave by a dreary-faced warrior. The Creator of men laid waste to this stronghold until the clamor of the citizens died away and the work of giants of old stood quite empty."

He who considered wisely the foundations of these walls and deeply pondered over this dark life with a discerning mind often recalled many combats long ago and spoke these words:

"Where is the horse now, and where is the young rider? Where is the ruler, the giver of treasure? Where are the seats at the banquet and the joys of the hall? Alas for the bright cup, and the warrior in his mail! Alas for the glory of the lord! How their time has departed, vanished under shades of night as if it had never been! Now there stands no trace of the band of comrades except a wall, wonderfully high, decorated with serpentine marks. Strong spears, weapons greedy for slaughter, destroyed the warriors—that was their glorious destiny. Now storms beat at the stony slopes and falling frost binds the earth. When darkness comes, the black shadow of night, wintry tumult sends bitter hail from the north in spite against mankind. All is wretched in the realms of earth. Here reward is fleeting; here friends are fleeting; here man is fleeting; here woman is fleeting. All the foundations of the earth grow useless."

Thus did the wise man reflect in his heart as he sat by himself, apart in meditation. Excellent is the man who maintains his faith. Such a one shall never be too quick to make known the bitterness of his heart unless he knows the remedy and can zealously bring it about. It shall be well for him who seeks grace and comfort from the Father in heaven, where a stronghold stands firm for us all.

The Battle of Maldon

Then he[1] ordered each young man to forsake his horse, to drive it far off and then advance, keeping his mind on the deeds of his hands and courageous resolution. When Offa's kinsman first understood the earl would not allow any to hang back, he let, then, his beloved hawk fly off from his hands far into the wood while he went forth to battle: by that token one could see the young man did not wish to prove soft in warfare when he took up his weapons. Eadric also wished to help his lord, his leader in the fight; he took up his spear and bore it for battle. His spirit was undaunted as long as he could hold shield and broadsword in his hands: he fulfilled his vow that he would fight before his lord.

Byrhtnoth now began to put his troops in order. He rode about and gave advice, instructing the warriors how they ought to stand and hold their position. He told them how to grasp their shields in the right way, firmly in their grip, and not to be afraid. When he had mustered all the people well, he lighted down in that place where he most wished to be, where he knew the loyal men of his own household were.

---

[1]"He" is Byrhtnoth, leader of the English army. Unfortunately, *The Battle of Maldon* is a fragment: both the beginning and the end have been lost.

A viking messenger now stood on the bank. Sternly he called out in measured words the message of the seafarers to the earl, there where he stood on the opposite shore: "Bold seamen sent me to you, bidding me to tell you that you must quickly send us treasure for protection. It will be better for you all to avoid the flight of spears by giving precious treasure rather than clashing in hard battle with us. We need not destroy each other if you have wealth enough: in exchange for gold, we wish to make a truce. If you advise this—you who count for most here—deciding that you wish to ransom your people, give the seamen whatever they demand, buy peace for the fee and receive a truce from us. Gladly will we take the treasure to our ships, putting off to sea and holding peace with you."

Byrhtnoth responded; raising his shield, he shook his slender spear. Measuring his words, resolute and angry, he gave him an answer: "Do you hear, seafarer, what this people says? They wish to give as tribute spears with deadly points, heirloom swords, battle gear which will not be of help to you in fighting. Viking messenger, go back and give your people much more hostile tidings! Here with his host stands a dauntless earl who wishes to defend this native land, Ethelred's realm, my lord's land and people. Heathens are about to fall in battle. It seems to me it would be a shame if you should take our tribute back to your ships without winning it in battle, now that you have come so far here into our land. It will not be quite so easy for you to gain treasure: spear point and sword edge in grim war shall decide the terms for us before we give you tribute."

Now he told the warriors to take up their shields and stand together on the riverbank. Nor could either army get to the other because of the water: flood tide came flowing there after the ebb and the sea-streams joined. It seemed to them too long a time before spears could clash. There on the banks of Panta's stream[2] they stood in proud array, the East Saxon troop and the viking army, nor could any of them harm the other, unless someone might be killed by a flying arrow.

The tide went out. The sailors stood ready, a throng of vikings ready for war. Then the warriors' leader ordered Wulfstan, a war-hardened veteran, to hold the causeway. Valiant as all his kindred—he was the son of Ceola—he struck down with his spear the first man bold enough to step onto the ford. By Wulfstan's side stood other fearless warriors, Alfhere and Maccus, two brave men who had no intention to flee from the ford but staunchly defended it against the enemies as long as they were able to make use of weapons.

When they understood that and could clearly see that they would find the guardians of the crossing fierce, the hateful intruders tried another tactic, asking for access, so that they might cross the ford and lead their army over. And, in his high pride, the leader undertook to allow too much land to the hateful people. Byrhthelm's son[3] called to them over the cold water and the men listened: "A way is opened for you now. Come quickly to us, men prepared for war. God alone knows who shall be master of this place of slaughter."

The sea wolves advanced—they did not shrink from water. The viking host came west over Panta, bearing shields over the glittering water; the seafaring men brought their spears to land. There against the fierce foe the men stood ready, Byrhtnoth with his warriors: he ordered his men to prepare the shield-wall and stand firmly against the enemies. Now the fight was near, glory to be won; now the time had come when doomed men would fall there dead. The battle cry was

---

[2]The River Blackwater, in Essex.
[3]I.e., Byrhtnoth.

raised. Ravens circled, and the eagle, eager to find carrion, as a cry came from the earth.

Hardened spears, grimly sharp weapons, flew from the warriors' hands. Bows were busy as points dug into shields. Bitter was the rush of battle as men fell on both sides, young warriors lying dead. Wulfmar was wounded: Byrhtnoth's kinsman, the son of his sister, chose a resting place among the slaughtered, cut down by the sword. But then the vikings were given due reward: I heard that Edward killed one with his sword. He did not hold back his strokes until the doomed warrior fell dead—for that, his lord thanked the chamberlain when he had the chance.

Thus the brave young men stood firm in battle, eagerly intent on who might be the first in taking the lives of the doomed with their weapons. The slain fell to the earth, but they stood resolute.

Byrhtnoth encouraged them, urging every young man to be intent on fighting if he wished to win fame at the Danes' expense. Strong in battle, he raised shield and weapons and advanced against a viking; the steadfast earl came up to the yeoman, each of them intending evil to the other. The seaman so sent a spear of southern make that the warriors' leader was given a wound, but he shoved back with his shield edge so that the shaft was shattered—it quivered and the spearhead fell out of the wound. The warrior was enraged and thrust at the proud viking who had given him that wound. The expert English fighter let his spear advance, guided by his hand, through the young man's neck, and pierced him fatally.

Then he quickly stabbed another so that his mail burst apart and he was wounded in the breast through the links of chain rings: in his heart the deadly point stopped. The earl was the happier. The brave man laughed and gave thanks to God that this day's work was granted him.

But then one of the vikings let a spear fly from his hands so that it went much too far through Ethelred's noble thane. By his side stood a youth not fully grown, a boy at the battle, who very valiantly drew out the bloody spear from the warrior's side; that young Wulfmar, son of Wulfstan, sent the hard spear back again. The point struck in so that he who had before so gravely wounded his own lord lay dead on the ground.

Now another armed man went toward the earl: he wanted to take the warrior's treasures, armor and rings and ornamented sword. Byrhtnoth drew his broad and gleaming blade from its sheath and struck at his mailcoat, but all too soon one of the vikings hampered him and maimed the earl's arm. The golden-hilted sword then fell to the ground, nor could he hold a hard blade in his hands or use weapons ever again. Still the gray-haired veteran found words to speak. He urged on the young men and all his comrades, though he could not much longer stand firmly on his feet.

He looked up to heaven: "I give thanks to you, Ruler of the heavens, for all the joys I have seen in this world. Merciful Creator, now I have great need that you may grant my spirit grace, so my soul may make its journey into your power in peace. Lord of the angels, I beseech you not to let the fiends of hell do it any harm."

Then heathen warriors cut him down, and both the men who stood by him, Alfnoth and Wulfmar, gave their lives beside their lord: both lay dead.

Those who did not wish to be there now left the battle. Odda's son Godric was the first in flight from war. Abandoning the good man who had so often given him many a fine horse, he mounted the steed which his lord had owned, leaping into trappings he had no right to use, and both his brothers, Godwin and Godwig, joined him in flight. They paid no heed to warfare and turned away from battle, seeking safety in the wood; they fled into the forest and safeguarded their lives, along with many more men than would have been fitting if they had remembered all the benefits their lord had given them. Offa once predicted, in the council hall, when men gathered together, that many a man there spoke courageously who later would not want to endure in time of need.

Now the people's leader, Ethelred's earl, had been laid low. All his close companions saw where their lord lay dead. The warlike thanes then pressed forward; undaunted, men hastened eagerly, for all of them wanted one of two fates: either to lose their lives or to avenge their lord. Thus the son of Alfric, a warrior young in years, spoke, encouraging their advance. Courageously he said, "Remember all the vows we raised in the mead-hall when seated on the benches we often pledged to do our part in battle. Now it can be seen who is truly brave. I wish all to know of my noble kindred and that I came from a great Mercian family; my grandfather, Ealhelm, was a wise chieftain blessed with worldly goods. Never shall the thanes among my people have cause to revile me, saying that I wanted to desert this army and seek my home, now that my leader lies cut down in battle. That is, to me, the greatest of griefs: he was both my kinsman and my lord."

Then he went forward, intent on striking back, and stabbed one of the seamen in the throng, leaving him on the ground cut down by his weapon, and he began to urge his neighbors, friends and comrades, to advance further.

Offa spoke now, shaking his spear: "Surely you, Alfwin, have reminded all the thanes of their duty. Now that our lord, the earl, lies on the ground, it is needful for us all for each to encourage every other warrior in the fighting as long as he can have and hold hard battle weapons, spear and sword. Godric has betrayed us all, cowardly son of Odda. All too many men saw him ride off on the fine war horse, and thought it was our lord: therefore the people on the field were divided and the shield-wall broken. May he come to a bad end when he has here caused so many men to flee!"

And he advanced angrily, fighting with determination—he scorned flight. Dunnere then spoke, shaking his spear; the simple yeoman called out to them all, urging every man to take vengeance for Byrhtnoth: "None may turn away who wishes to avenge his lord on the enemy, nor may he worry about saving his own life!"

They pressed forward, heedless of their lives. The band of retainers, bitter spear-bearers, fought on fiercely, praying to God that they might avenge their lord and bring about the fall of their enemies. A hostage most willingly came to their aid. He was called Ashferth, Ecglaf's son, and came of a hardy Northumbrian clan. He did not flinch at all from the war-play, but continually shot arrows forth: now he shot into a shield, now he pierced a man, and now and again he gave someone a wound as long as he was able to bear weapons.

Still at the forefront stood Edward the tall. Ready and most eager, he made his vow that he would not give way so much as a foot; never would he turn back there where his leader lay. He broke through the shield-wall and fought against those warriors until he had worthily avenged his lord on the seafarers before he lay among the slaughtered. Like him, Ethelric, the noble retainer, was eager to advance and fought in grim earnest; Sigebyrht's brother and many others, too, cleft through shields and defended themselves boldly.

Shield rims burst, and shattered mail sang a song of terror. In the fighting there, Offa cut down a viking attacker who fell to the ground, but Gadd's kinsman also fell: Offa was quickly cut down in battle. He fulfilled the vows he had made to his lord when he had earlier promised his patron that either they would both ride safely to the manor or both fall in war, destroyed by wounds on the place of slaughter. He lay as a noble thane should, near his lord.

Again shields clashed and the vikings advanced, enraged, in the battle; many a spear passed through a doomed body. Then Wistan went forward, Thurstan's son, fighting with the enemy. He killed three in the midst of the throng before Wighelm's kinsman lay among the slaughtered. The battle raged. Warriors stood firm in the struggle while others fell, weary with wounds. Oswold and Eadwold all the while encouraged the men; both the brothers urged their friends and kinsmen to hold fast there in time of need, to make use of weapons without faltering.

Now an old retainer, Byrhtwold, spoke. Lifting up his shield and shaking his spear, he courageously told the men, "Courage shall be firmer, heart all the keener, spirit the greater, as our might grows less. Here lies our leader, fatally cut down, the good man in the dust. Forever shall that man mourn who now thinks to leave the battle! I am far advanced in years and I shall not leave. I intend to lie by the side of my dear lord."

So also did Godric, Ethelgar's son, call them all to battle. Again and again he bore down on the vikings with his deadly spear as he fought in the forefront of the people, striking and cutting down, until he fell in battle. That was not the Godric who fled from the fight . . .

The Seafarer

I shall tell you a true tale about myself: speak of my journeys, and how I have often endured days of toil in time of hardship. I have known bitter care in my breast, found many a place where care dwells on deck over the terrible tossing waves; often have I held the anxious night watch, there at the prow of a ship beating along cliffs. My feet were pinched with cold, bound in the cold grip of frost, as searing hot sorrows sighed around my heart and hunger tore from within at my sea-weary spirit.

All this is unknown to the man for whom all goes most beautifully on land. He little thinks how I, miserable with cares, kept to the paths of exile through the winter on the ice-cold sea, deprived of friends and kinsmen—hung about with icicles, while hail fell in showers around me. There I heard nothing but the roaring sea, the ice-cold wave. At times the song of the wild swan had to do as my entertainment, the call of the gannet and the cry of the curlew for men's laughter, and the singing gull for the drinking of mead. Storms battered the cliffs, where the icy-feathered tern often answered the damp-feathered eagle's scream. No protecting kinsmen could comfort the destitute soul.

He who has known the joy of life in the dwellings of men, he who, standing proud and gladdened with

wine, has had few[1] bitter journeys: he cannot believe
how I, in my weariness, have often had to endure on
the paths of the sea. The shadow of night grew dark.
Snow came from the north and frost bound the ground,
while hail, the coldest of grains, fell on the ground. Yet
indeed now thoughts beat at my heart that I should
know the high seas myself, the crashing of the salty
waves: desire of spirit constantly urges my heart to go
forth to seek the home of strangers far away from
here.[2] For there is no man on earth so proud of spirit,
nor so generously gifted, nor so spurred by youth or
brave in deeds or dear to his lord that he shall always
have no anxious thought for his voyage.

Then his thought is not on harping or on receiving
rings: his delight is not in women or in worldly bliss, or
anything else at all unless it is the tossing waves. He
who is impelled to set out on the sea is always restless
with longing. The groves burst into blossom and make
the dwelling-places beautiful and the meadows fair.
The world moves along. All these urge the eager spirit
and the heart to its journey in one who indeed intends
to depart along the far ways of the sea. Thus the
cuckoo urges in sad song: summer's herald sings, fore-
boding bitter sorrow in the breast. A warrior blessed
with comfort does not know what some then endure
who lie most far away on the paths of exile.

Thus my mind now turns beyond the confines of
my breast, and my thoughts turn widely with the flow-
ing sea, over the home of whales and the surfaces of
the world; it comes back to me eager and full of
longing—the lone flier cries out irresistibly, inciting
the heart forth on the whale's road, over the boundless
sea, for to me the joys of the Lord are warmer by far
than this dead and transitory life on land. I do not

---

[1] An example of *litotes*: take "few" as meaning "none at all."
[2] This may suggest heaven; cf. end of poem, and see *Hebrews* 11:13–16, e.g.

believe that earthly riches will stand firm for them forever. One of the three things always lies in wait for each retainer before his time is done: illness or old age or the sword of an enemy wrests life away from the man doomed to go forth. Therefore for every nobleman the best of reputations is glory given by the living speaking of him afterwards. This he can earn before he must take his way, through action on earth against every foe, brave deeds against the devil, so that he may afterwards be praised by the sons of men and his glory then live among the angels to eternity: eternal fruit of life, joy among the host.

The days have departed, all the pomp of earthly realms; nor are kings and emperors and the givers-of-gold now as they once were, when they brought about among them the most great of glorious deeds and lived in lordly renown. All that host has fallen, and their joys have departed. The lesser remain and hold this world, toiling to make use of it. The fruit is brought low, the excellence of earth withers and decays, just as does every man now everywhere on earth. Age comes upon him and his face grows wan; the gray-haired man laments, knowing that his dear friend, the son of noblemen, has been given to the ground. His fleshly dwelling cannot, when it has lost its life, taste any sweetness or feel any sore, lift up a hand or think with a mind. Though a brother may strew gold on his sibling's grave, bury all sorts of treasure with the dead, they shall not go with him; nor can gold, which he hoarded before while he still lived here, be of help to the soul full of sins against the wrath of God.

Great is the wrath of the Creator, for the earth turns away from it. He made the firm grounds, the surfaces of the earth, and the heavens above. Foolish is he who does not dread his Lord: death comes upon him unexpectedly. Blessed is he who lives in humbleness: grace shall come to him from heaven. The Creator made him firm in spirit, for he believed in his might. A man must steer a strong spirit and keep it firm and constant to its undertakings and pure in its ways.

Every man should keep moderation in his love for those he cares for and in his malice towards those he hates, even if he sees one unjustly rewarded or a dear friend destroyed on a pyre. Destiny is stronger, and the Maker mightier, than any man conceives. Let us consider where we have a home, and then how we may come thither; and let us so endeavor that we may go to that eternal blessedness where there is endless life in the love of the Lord, bliss in heaven. May the Holy One be thanked for that: that he, Father of glory, the eternal Lord, so honored us for all time.

The Seafarer

Translated by Ezra Pound[1]

May I for my own self song's truth reckon,
Journey's jargon, how I in harsh days
Hardship endured oft.
Bitter breast-cares have I abided,
Known on my keel many a care's hold,
And dire sea-urge, and there I oft spent
Narrow nightwatch nigh the ship's head
While she tossed close to cliffs. Coldly afflicted,
My feet were by frost benumbed.
Chill its chains are; chafing sighs
Hew my heart round and hunger begot
Mere-weary mood. Lest man know not
That he on dry land loveliest liveth,
List how I, care-wretched, on ice-cold sea,
Weathered the winter, wretched outcast
Deprived of my kinsmen;
Hung with hard ice-flakes, where hail-scur flew,
There I heard naught save the harsh sea
And ice-cold wave, at whiles the swan cries,
Did for my games the gannet's clamour,

[1]From Ezra Pound, *Personae*. Copyright 1926 by Ezra Pound. Reprinted by permission of New Directions Publishing Corporation.

Sea-fowls' loudness was for me laughter
The mews' singing all my mead-drink.
Storms, on the stone-cliffs beaten, fell on the stern
In icy feathers; full oft the eagle screamed
With spray on his pinion

                                   Not any protector
May make merry man faring needy.
This he little believes, who aye in winsome life
Abides 'mid burghers some heavy business,
Wealthy and wine-flushed, how I weary oft
Must abide above brine
Neareth nightshade, snoweth from north,
Frost froze the land, hail fell on earth then,
Corn of the coldest. Nathless there knocketh now
The heart's thought that I on high streams
The salt-wavy tumult traverse alone.
Moaneth alway my mind's lust
That I fare forth, that I afar hence
Seek out a foreign fastness
For this there's no mood-lofty man over earth's midst,
Not though he be given his good, but will have in his
    youth greed;
Nor his deed to the daring, nor his king to the faithful
But shall have his sorrow for sea-fare
Whatever his lord will.
He hath not heart for harping, nor in ring-having
Nor winsomeness to wife, nor world's delight
Nor any whit else save the wave's slash,
Yet longing comes upon him to fare forth on the water.
Bosque taketh blossom, cometh beauty of berries,
Fields to fairness, land fares brisker,
All this admonisheth man eager of mood,
The heart turns to travel so that he then thinks
On flood-ways to be far departing.
Cuckoo calleth with gloomy crying,
He singeth summerward, bodeth sorrow,
The bitter heart's blood. Burgher knows not—

He the prosperous man—what some perform
Where wandering them widest draweth.
So that but now my heart burst from my breastlock,
My mood 'mid the mere-flood,
Over the whale's acre, would wander wide.
On earth's shelter cometh oft to me,
Eager and ready, the crying lone-flyer,
Whets for the whale-path the heart irresistibly,
O'er tracks of ocean; seeing that anyhow
My lord deems to me this dead life
On loan and on land, I believe not
That any earth-weal eternal standeth
Save there be somewhat calamitous
That, ere a man's tide go, turn it to twain.
Disease or oldness or sword-hate
Beats out the breath from doom-gripped body.
And for this, every earl whatever, for those speaking
    after—
Laud of the living, boasteth some last word,
That he will work ere he pass onward,
Frame on the fair earth 'gainst foes his malice,
Daring ado, . . .
So that all men shall honour him after
And his laud beyond them remain 'mid the English,
Aye, for ever, a lasting life's blast,
Delight 'mid the doughty.
                                    Days little durable,
And all the arrogance of earthen riches,
There come now no kings nor Caesars
Nor gold-giving lords like those gone.
Howe'er in earth most magnified,
Whoe'er lived in life most lordliest,
Drear all this excellence, delights undurable!
Waneth the watch, but the world holdeth.
Tomb hideth trouble. The blade is layed low.
Earthly glory ageth and seareth.
No man at all going the earth's gait,

The Seafarer

But age fares against him, his face paleth,
Grey-haired he groaneth, knows gone companions,
Lordly men, are to earth o'ergiven,
Nor may he then the flesh-cover, whose life ceaseth,
Nor eat the sweet nor feel the sorry,
Nor stir hand nor think in mid heart,
And though he strew the grave with gold,
His born brothers, their buried bodies
Be an unlikely treasure hoard.[2]

---

[2]Pound omits the specifically Christian conclusion of the poem (thought by some scholars to be an epilogue—like *The Wanderer*, *The Seafarer* can be interpreted as representing more than one speaker), just as within the body of the poem, he has changed or eliminated references to God, the afterlife, etc.

Judith

Judith did not doubt the gifts of God in this wide world.[1] The glorious Lord made a refuge ready for her when she had greatest need for the highest Judge's grace: creation's Ruler gave her protection from the highest terror. The sublime mind of the Father in heaven granted her this boon because she had always had firm faith in the Almighty.

It is told that Holofernes eagerly prepared a splendid banquet, magnificent in every way, and then the prince of men sent for all of his chief thanes to drink wine with him. The warriors obeyed in great haste and came to the mighty lord, leader of the people. This was on the fourth day since wise-minded Judith, a lady lovely as an elf, first came to him. The proud men went to their seats; all that woeful company of bold armed warriors sat down to the wine drinking. Deep bowls were carried often down the benches with full cups and pitchers for those who sat in the hall. The famous fighting men drank doomed to death—though the mighty and terrible lord of the noblemen did not expect that.

Holofernes, generous patron of men, rejoiced as

---

[1]Since the fragment we have of this poem begins in mid-sentence, only a few words here have manuscript authority.

wine was poured. He laughed and he roared, he shouted and raised such a din that the sons of men could hear from far away how the strong-minded leader stormed and yelled, bold and flushed with mead, as he kept on urging the guests on the bench to disport themselves. And thus the whole day long the wicked man, strong-minded treasure-giver, drenched his troops with wine until they fell in a swoon: all that host was so overcome with wine that they lay as if they had been struck down by death, drained of all good.

Thus the prince of warriors ordered his guests in the hall to be filled with drink until the shadows of night grew near the sons of men. Then the evildoer ordered that the noble lady, adorned with rings and decked with rich treasure, be fetched to his bed at once. Quickly the retainers did as their chieftain, ruler of the warriors, had commanded, and noisily advanced to the guest quarters. There they found Judith, wise in spirit. Without delay the armed band began to lead the sublime maid to the high pavilion, where mighty Holofernes—hateful to the Savior—always went to rest at night.

Over the commander's bed hung a lovely curtain of golden fly netting; through it the baleful prince of warriors might look and see any of the sons of men who came there, yet none of the race of men could see him himself, unless that bold man, confirmed in evil, should order a warrior to come nearer to take counsel. Promptly, then, they brought the wise lady to this resting place, and then, firm in spirit, the men let their lord know that the hallowed woman had been brought to his pavilion. The famous lord of the dwellings was made joyful: he intended to defile that bright lady filthily and foully. But the Judge in his majesty, Guardian of glory, would not suffer that to be: the Lord God of hosts prevented this deed.

The demonic lecher left his troop of men to find

his bed, with wicked intent: there he was to lose his glory before the night was past. The strong-minded lord of men had reached the cruel end of his life on earth that he deserved, according to the deeds he had performed while he dwelled here under heaven's roof. The mighty one fell upon his resting place so drunk with wine that his wits were quite devoid of wisdom. The warriors left the chamber in great haste; men drunk with wine, they had led the hateful tyrant to his bed for the last time.

The Savior's glorious handmaiden then considered carefully how she might most easily take the terrible man's life before that impure sinner should awake. The curly-haired lady, maid of the Creator, grasped a sharp sword, hardened in battle, and drew it from its sheath with her right hand. She made her prayer to the Guardian of heaven, calling on the name of the Savior of all who dwell on earth and saying these words: "God of creation and Spirit of comfort, Son of the Ruler—I beg you to have mercy on me in my need, glorious Trinity! My heart is on fire and my mind is troubled, burdened with great sorrow. Ruler of heaven, grant me victory and true faith, that with this sword I may cut down this murder-giver. Grant me salvation, strong-minded Lord of men: never have I had greater need of your mercy. Now, mighty Lord, sublime Giver of glory, avenge the grief of my mind and the hatred in my breast!"

And at once the highest Judge inspired her with courage, as he will anyone on earth who wisely seeks his help in true faith. Then her mind was lightened, holy hope renewed. She took the heathen man firmly by the hair and drew him towards her with her hands, putting him to shame; skillfully she placed the wicked, hateful man so that she could deal most easily with that wretched creature. The curly-haired lady struck the baleful enemy with her hostile sword, and cut halfway through his neck as he lay there in a swoon, drunk and sorely wounded. But he was not as yet quite dead and lifeless; for the second time, then, the valiant lady earnestly struck the heathen hound, and the head rolled off on the floor. The foul corpse lay there empty while the spirit departed into the dark abyss, where it was weighed down in painful punishment for ever after, wound about with serpents, bound in torments, firmly imprisoned in the flames of hell after its departure. Enveloped in darkness, he had no cause to hope that he might escape the den of serpents. There he must stay for ever and ever, world without end, in the dark dwelling where there is no hope or joy.

Judith had achieved great glory in battle, as God, the Lord of heaven, had granted her when he gave her victory. The wise maid swiftly picked up the warrior's bloody head and put it in the sack in which her pale-cheeked attendant, a virtuous lady, had brought food there for them both. Judith gave the gory burden to her prudent handmaid to be carried home. The two courageous women then proceeded from that place until the joyful and triumphant maids had come out of the encampment of the invading army and they could clearly see the shining walls of the lovely city of Bethulia. Both beautifully adorned, they hurried on the roadway until they had come with gladness to the city gate. There warriors were stationed, alert men keeping watch over the stronghold, as Judith, the keen-witted maid, had ordered the anxious people when that valiant lady went on her journey.

Now she had returned, dear to her people, and the wise-minded woman swiftly told one of the men from the great city to come to her and let her in at once through the gate in the wall. She spoke these words to the triumphant people: "I bring you tidings worthy of thanksgiving: that you need mourn no longer. The Creator, most glorious of kings, has been gracious to you. It has been made manifest throughout the world that you shall now be given great glory and supreme success in place of the affliction you have long suffered."

Those who dwelled in the city rejoiced when they heard the words of the holy one over the high wall. The host was overjoyed and the people hurried to the gates of the fortress—men and women together in great multitudes, companies and troops, thronged and ran to the Lord's maid by the thousandfold, both young and old. The spirits of everyone in the city soared when they learned that Judith had returned to her home: with great reverence, they quickly let her in.

The wise one, in her gold adornments, then told her attentive handmaid to reveal the warrior's head and show it to the people of the city as a bloody token of her success in battle. The noble lady spoke to all the people: "Here, triumphant warriors, leaders of the people, you may gaze at the head of dead Holofernes, most hateful of heathens, who brought about many murders of our men, terrible sorrows to us, and intended to add to them. But God did not grant him longer life in which to afflict us with further harm. With God's help, I took his life. Now I wish to call upon each man of the city, every armed warrior, to prepare for battle right away. As soon as God the Father, the gracious King, sends bright light from the east, bring forth your spears, your shields before your breasts in your coats of mail: bear your bright helmets into the midst of the enemy and strike down their commanders, ill-fated chieftains, with your hostile swords. Your enemies are doomed to death, and you shall win fame and glory in battle. This the mighty Lord has shown you through my hand!"

A band of bold men was soon prepared, keen for battle. A troop of noble warriors and their comrades advanced, bearing triumphal banners: men in helmets went straight out to battle from the holy city at the break of day. Their shields raised a din, resounding loudly. The lank wolf of the wood heard and rejoiced, and the dark raven, greedy for carrion. They both knew that the warriors meant to give them their fill of doomed men. Behind them flew the dewy-winged eagle, eager for prey; the dusky-coated bird sang a battle song with its horny beak.

The warriors advanced, men bound for battle behind shields of hollow wood. Before this they had suffered the insults of foreigners, the abuse of the heathens—now the Assyrians were thoroughly repaid in the spear-play when the Hebrews under their war standards came into their camp. Promptly they let fly showers of arrows, strong stinging missiles flying from their bows. Loudly the fierce warriors stormed as they sent their hard spears into the throng—the men of the land were enraged at the hated foe and advanced sternly. Firm in spirit, urgently they aroused their old enemies, weary with mead. Pulling gaily ornamented swords with well-tried edges from their sheaths, the retainers struck hard at the evil Assyrians, sparing no one of the enemy army, whether high or low: they left no man alive whom they could overcome.

Thus throughout the morning the noble thanes pursued the foreigners until the leaders of the invading host saw quite clearly how fierce they were, and that the Hebrew men were giving out hard sword strokes. They went to take word to their chief leaders: in fear they aroused the mead-weary warriors, announcing the dreadful tidings of the morning's terror and the frightful play of weapons. Then, it is said, the doomed men shook off sleep and with weary spirits thronged to the pavilion of baleful Holofernes. They meant to tell their lord about the battle quickly, before the terror of the Hebrews fell upon him.

All of them thought the lecherous prince of warriors, terrible and fierce, was in the lovely tent together with the bright lady, noble Judith: nor was there any nobleman there who dared to wake the warrior or inquire how the commander had fared with the Creator's handmaid, the holy woman. The host grew nearer and the Hebrew people fought sternly on with deadly hard weapons, fiercely repaying all their former conflict with their hostile swords. The fame of Assyria was lessened by that day's work, its pride brought low. In great agitation, the men stood around their lord's pavilion, somber in spirit. All together they began to cough; they cried out aloud and gnashed their teeth—lacking any good, they suffered to their teeth. Their glory had now come to an end: gone were their success and their deeds of valor. The noblemen meant to arouse their lord; but they did not succeed.

Then at long last one of the warriors became bold enough to venture daringly inside the pavilion, driven by necessity. There he found his generous patron lying on the bed—pale, empty, and deprived of life. At once he fell down trembling to the floor and began to tear his hair and clothes in agony of mind. He said to the downcast warriors standing outside, "Our own destruction has clearly come upon us. Here it can be seen that the time has come when affliction draws near and we shall all be lost—together we shall perish in battle. Here lies our leader, cut down by the sword, beheaded."

With agonized minds, they threw down their weapons and, weary in spirit, departed from that place, scattering in flight. The mighty tribe followed them, fighting on, until the greater part of the invading army lay destroyed in battle on the field of victory: they were cut down by the sword and left for the enjoyment of the wolves and the pleasure of birds eager for carrion. Those of the hateful army who were still alive fled, with the troops of the Hebrews close on their tracks, glorious in victory—they had won fame with the help of the Lord God, the almighty Father. Boldly the valiant warriors used their hostile swords to cut a path through the hateful throng, splitting shields and cutting through the shield-wall. The Hebrew host fought in furious rage—thanes most eager for the meeting of spears—and there in the dust fell the greater part of the noblest war-band of the hated Assyrians. Few returned alive to their native land.

The brave warriors turned back on their way home, tracing their way among the reeking corpses. The men of that country did not lack opportunity to take blood-stained spoils from the hated enemy, and from their dead foes they gathered lovely ornaments, shields and broadswords, shining helmets and valuable treasures. The defenders of the homeland had gloriously defeated their enemies on the battlefield, laying their old foes to rest with their swords—those who had been most hateful to them of all living peoples lay where they had fallen. For a full month the curly-haired tribe, most renowned of nations, carried off helmets, shining mail and daggers, warriors' weapons decorated with gold, and more splendid treasures than any tongue can tell, into the bright city of Bethulia. The bold warriors won all this on the battlefield under their banners through the wise counsel of the daring maid Judith.

And, as her own reward from the journey, the brave noblemen brought to her the sword of Holofernes, his bloody helmet and his ample mail adorned with red gold, and all the strong-minded prince of men had owned of treasure or of heirlooms, rings and bright jewels: all this they gave to the bright, quick-witted lady. For this Judith gave glory to the Lord of hosts, who granted her honor and glory here on earth as well as a heavenly reward, triumph in heaven above, because she had firm faith in the Almighty. She never doubted that in the end she would have the reward for which she had long yearned.

For this, glory be to the dear Lord for ever and ever, world without end—to him who in his mercy created wind and air, the heavens and the wide world, the raging waters and the joys of heaven.

The Fight at Finnsburh[1]

The young king, survivor of few battles, then called out, "This is not the day breaking in the east, nor is there a fiery dragon flying here—nor are the gabled horns of this hall burning. But the birds of prey are singing here and the gray wolf howls. Wooden war-weapons speak out noisily, shield answers spear-shaft. The moon shines fitfully now through the clouds, and now dreadful deeds arise, with intent to bring evil on our people. Awake now, my warriors, have your shields ready: be of good courage and turn to the front with steadfast resolve!"

Many a thane arose then, in his golden ornaments, girding on his sword. To the door went noble champions, Sigeferth and Eaha, with drawn swords, and at the other door, Ordlaf and Guthlaf, with Hengest himself following in their footsteps.

Garulf urged Guthere not to risk his noble life by going in his fine trappings to the hall door when one hard in enmity wished to destroy him; but he called out dauntlessly over them all and asked who held the door.

---

[1] This fragment of verse tells, in a very different way, part of the story used by the *Beowulf*-poet in the "Finnsburh episode." The language, syntax, and even personnel are all quite confusing: thus certain aspects of the translation are, inevitably, rather arbitrary.

"My name is Sigeferth, a man of the Secgan tribe: a well-known wanderer, I have known much trouble and come through bitter battles. You will soon enough know what you can gain from me!"

The noise of deadly slaughter was heard in the hall. Wooden shields burst in the hands of keen warriors and floorboards of the hall resounded in the din, until Garulf fell in battle: Guthlaf's son was first to die of the natives of that land. Around him many good men fell as the raven circled, dark and dusky-coated.

Light flashed from swords as if all Finnsburh were afire. Never have I heard of sixty staunch warriors who bore themselves in battle more honorably, nor have retainers ever better repaid their mead than Hnaef's young warriors paid him for theirs. For five days the band of companions fought and held the door: and none of them was killed.

Then a wounded warrior turned to go away, saying that his coat of mail, strong war-gear, had been shattered, and his helmet pierced. The leader of the people quickly asked him how the warriors fared with their wounds, and whether the young men . . .

Appendixes
and
Bibliography

Appendix A

Beowulf, Lines 26–52, in Old English

The spelling of the passage on the following page has been partially "normalized" for consistency. E.g., the two sounds spelled *th* in Modern English are differentiated: þ is used for the sound heard in *thin* and *bath*, and ð for the sound in *then* and *bathe*. For manuscript spelling, see Klaeber's text, or that of Dobbie or Wrenn, as listed in the Bibliography, p. 145.

On the page facing the passage is a phonetic transcription, intended to be rendered according to standard American English pronunciation for the given spellings, for the convenience of those who are unfamiliar with the International Phonetic Alphabet. The careful reader should come close enough if he tries to stress only the syllables marked [/], indicating primary stress, and [\], indicating secondary (but almost as strong) stress. Syllable divisions for words of more than one syllable are indicated with hyphens, but note that some syllables (such as *beya*) are practically disyllabic. Dots indicate a slight pause. To achieve a rhythmic reading, give each of the four syllable-groups (indicated by spacing) of a line approximately equal time (cf. Introduction, p. xvi).

A literal prose translation of the passage appears on page 142.

139

Beowulf Text

Him þā Scyld ȝewāt to ȝescæphwīle
felahrōr feran on Frēan wǣre;
hī hine þā ætbǣron tō brimes faroðe,
swǣse ȝesīðas, swā hē selfa bæd,
þenden wordum wēold wine Scyldinga—
!ēof landfruma lange āhte.
Þǣr æt hȳðe stōd hringedstefna
īsiȝ ond ūtfūs, æðelinges fær;
ālēdon þā lēofne þēoden,
bēaga bryttan on bearm scipes,
mǣrne be mæste. Þǣr wæs māðma fela
of feorweȝum frætwa ȝelǣded;
ne hȳrde ic cȳmlīcor cēol ȝeȝyrwan
hildewǣpnum ond heaðowǣdum,
billum ond byrnum; him on bearme læȝ
māðma mænigo, þā him mid scoldon
on flōdes ǣht feor ȝewītan.
Nalæs hī hine lǣssan lācum tēodan,
þēodȝestrēonum, þon þā dydon,
þē hine æt frumsceafte forþ onsendon
ǣnne ofer ȳðe umborwesende.
Þā ȝȳt hīe him āsetton seȝen gyldenne
hēah ofer hēafod, lēton holm beran,
ȝēafon on gārsecg; him wæs ȝēomor sefa,
murnende mōd. Men ne cunnon
secgan tō sōðe, selerǣdende,
hæleþ under heofenum, hwā bǣm hlæste onfēng.

Phonetic Transcription

.. Him thah Shield yuh-wot .. toe yuh- shap-wheel-uh
fel-a-hrore fare-on on Frayan wear-uh
he hin-uh thah at- bare-on toe brim-is far-othe-uh
swy-za yuh- seethe-es .. swah hay sel-va bad
.. then-din wor-dum wayld win-uh Shield-ing-ga.
layf . lond-frum-a long-guh okt-uh.
.. There at heethe-uh stode hring-ged stev-na
eez-y ond oot-foos ath-el-ing-gus far ..
ah-lay-don thah .. layv-nuh thayo-den .
beya-ga brit-ton .. on bearm ship-is .
mare-nuh bey mast-uh .. There was mahthe-ma fel-a
... of fare-way-um frat-wa yuh- lad-ed.
nuh heer-duh ich keem-leek-or tchayol yuh- yeer-wan
hil-duh- wap-num ond hathe-o way-dum .
bil-lum ond beer-num .. him on bearm-uh lay
mahthe-ma men-i-go .. thah him mid shol-don
... on flode-is akt fare yuh- weet-on.
Nah-les he hin-uh lase-son lah-kum tayo-don
thayo-dya- strayo-num ... thon thah did-on
they hin-uh at frum-shaft-uh forth on- send-on
ann-nuh over euthe-uh . umb'r- wez-end-uh.
Thah yeet he-uh him ah- set-ton sey-yen gil-den-nuh
hayac over haya-vod .. lay-ton holm ber-on.
yayve-on on gar-sedge .. him was yo-mor se-va .
moor-nin-duh mode .. Men nuh kun-non
sedge-on toe sothe-uh . sel-a- rad-en-duh
hal-eth un-der heh-ven-um .. hwah tham hlast-uh on-feng.

Translation

Then Scyld departed at [the] fated time, [the] very strong [man], [to] go into [the] keeping [of the] Lord; they then bore him to [the] sea's current, dear companions, as he himself bade, when [the] friendly lord [of the] Scyldings wielded words—[the] dear land's prince ruled long. There at harbor waited [a] ring-prowed [ship], icy and eager to set out, [a] prince's vessel; [they] laid down there [their] dear lord, [the] giver [of] rings, in [the] bosom [of the] ship, [the] glorious [one] by the mast. There were brought many treasures, ornaments, from far ways; nor have I heard [of a] ship more beautifully equipped [with] battle-weapons and war-garments, swords and byrnies; on his bosom lay many treasures, which should go far with him in [the] power [of the] flood. Not at all did they give him lesser gifts, nation's treasures, than did those who in [the] beginning sent him forth alone over [the] waves as a child. Then besides they placed [a] golden banner high over [his] head, let [the] sea take [him], gave [him] into [the] ocean; their spirit was sad, mood mournful. Men could not say certainly, hall-counselors, warriors under [the] heavens, who received that load.

Appendix B

Genealogical Tables

THE DANES

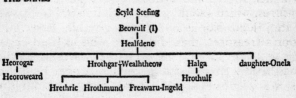

THE GEATS

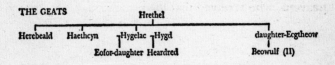

THE SWEDES

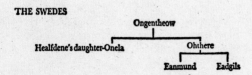

Bibliography

An illuminating and commendably concise book on *Beowulf* which can be recommended to all readers of the poem is T. A. Shippey's *Beowulf* (London: Arnold, 1978); another useful introductory book is Edward B. Irving's *An Introduction to Beowulf* (Englewood Cliffs, N. J.: Prentice-Hall, 1969). But the first place to look for further specific information about the poem is the edition in Old English edited by Friedrich Klaeber (New York: D. C. Heath & Co., 3rd ed., 1950). The introduction, notes, bibliographies, and other apparatus will assist any serious inquirer, whether or not he reads Old English. C. L. Wrenn's edition of the poem (London: Harrap, 3rd ed. revised by W. F. Bolton, 1973) also contains useful apparatus, but of a more limited nature. A major collection of historical, literary, and archeological backgrounds is R. W. Chambers's *Beowulf, an Introduction to the Study of the Poem* (with supplement by C. L. Wrenn; Cambridge: The University Press, 3rd ed., 1959).

Judith is included in the volume *Beowulf and Judith* edited by Elliott van Kirk Dobbie (Vol. IV of *The Anglo-Saxon Poetic Records*; New York: Columbia University Press, 1953) and in a separate edition edited by B. J. Timmer (London: Methuen & Co., 2nd ed., 1961). *The Finnsburh Fragment*, of special interest to students of

Beowulf, is printed in most Old English editions of that poem and in a separate edition edited by Donald K. Fry (London: Methuen, 1974). A well-annotated text containing all the other shorter poems in the present volume is John C. Pope's *Seven Old English Poems* (New York: W. W. Norton, 2nd ed., 1981). Pope gives complete information about previous editions of the poems he includes.

The most readable standard history of the Anglo-Saxon period is Peter Hunter Blair, *An Introduction to Anglo-Saxon England* (Cambridge: The University Press, 1962). Other volumes containing valuable background information on the period are Dorothy Whitelock, *The Beginnings of English Society* (London: Penguin, 1952); R. I. Page, *Life in Anglo-Saxon England* (London: Batsford, 1970; copiously illustrated); and, of special value for students of literature, Milton McC. Gatch, *Loyalties and Traditions: Man and His World in Old English Literature* (New York: Pegasus, 1971).

A good survey of Old English literature in general is Stanley B. Greenfield, *A Critical History of Old English Literature* (New York: New York University Press, 1965). Greenfield's *The Interpretation of Old English Poetry* (London: Routledge & Kegan Paul, 1972) is also valuable, as is Shippey's *Old English Verse* (London: Hutchinson, 1972). Some important essays will be found in Jess B. Bessinger, Jr., and Stanley Kahrl, eds., *Essential Articles for the Study of Old English Poetry* (Hamden, Conn.: Archon, 1968); Donald K. Fry, ed., *The Beowulf-Poet, a Collection of Critical Essays* (Englewood Cliffs, N. J.: Prentice-Hall, 1968); Lewis E. Nicholson, ed., *An Anthology of Beowulf Criticism* (Notre Dame, Indiana: Notre Dame University Press, 1963); and Martin Stevens and Jerome Mandel, eds., *Old English Literature: 22 Analytical Essays* (Lincoln, Nebraska: University of Nebraska Press, 1968).

For those interested in reading more medieval Germanic literature, much is available in translation. The greatest of the Icelandic sagas, *Njal's Saga,* trans. Magnús Magnússon and Hermann Pálsson (Baltimore: Penguin, 1960) is only one of many recent saga translations. *The Nibelungenlied,* trans. A. T. Hatto (Baltimore: Penguin, 1965) has an illuminating "Introduction to a Second Reading." Interesting examples of Celtic literature of the "heroic" period can be found in *The Mabinogi and Other Medieval Welsh Tales,* trans. Patrick K. Ford (Berkeley: The University of California Press, 1977) and *The Tain,* trans. Thomas Kinsella (London: Oxford University Press, 1970). Old French epic poetry also has a lot in common with German heroic poetry: it is best represented in *The Song of Roland,* which is available in a number of readable translations.

A Note on the Cover

Sutton Hoo, an estate in Suffolk, England, is the site of one of the richest Germanic burials found in Europe, containing the remains of an eighty-five–foot long ship built for thirty-eight rowers and fully equipped for the afterlife. Ship burial, a widespread custom during the seventh and eighth centuries A.D., centered around the myth of the god-hero who sails away from his people in death, promising to return again. Sutton Hoo, the most famous of such ship burials, contained forty-one items of solid gold, including gold-mounted weapons and armor, buckles, strap mounts, buttons, a pair of lavishly decorated epaulets, a quantity of silverware, silver bowls and cups, and a magnificent gold purse lid decorated with seven ornamental plaques.

The cover of this book reproduces, by kind permission of the British Museum, one of these ornamental plaques. The detail, of a warrior between two beasts, is an example of the cloisonné technique, in which thin strips of metal are shaped into decorative patterns and attached, in this case, to the gold base of the object. Then enamel, mosaic glass, and jewels are laid into each section of the design and polished to add brilliance. The Sutton Hoo purse lid is Anglo-Saxon and probably dates back to the first quarter of the seventh century A.D.

Bantam Classics bring you the world's greatest literature—books that have stood the test of time—at specially low prices. These beautifully designed books will be proud additions to your bookshelf. You'll want all these time-tested classics for your own reading pleasure.

Titles by Mark Twain:

☐ 21079-3	**ADVENTURES OF HUCKLEBERRY FINN**	$2.50
☐ 21128-5	**ADVENTURES OF TOM SAWYER**	$2.25
☐ 21195-1	**COMPLETE SHORT STORIES**	$5.95
☐ 21143-9	**A CONNECTICUT YANKEE IN KING ARTHUR'S COURT**	$3.50
☐ 21349-0	**LIFE ON THE MISSISSIPPI**	$2.50
☐ 21256-7	**THE PRINCE AND THE PAUPER**	$2.25
☐ 21158-7	**PUDD'NHEAD WILSON**	$2.50

Other Great Classics:

☐ 21274-5	**BILLY BUDD** Herman Melville	$2.95
☐ 21311-3	**MOBY DICK** Herman Melville	$3.50
☐ 21233-8	**THE CALL OF THE WILD & WHITE FANG** Jack London	$2.95
☐ 21011-4	**THE RED BADGE OF COURAGE** Stephen Crane	$1.95
☐ 21350-4	**THE COUNT OF MONTE CRISTO** Alexander Dumas	$4.95